SEEK

TALES OF QUESTS AND ADVENTURES

edited by
Elin Korund

TABLE OF CONTENTS

FOREWORD

Escapist fantasies are sometimes maligned as childish and lacking in real-world value, however I believe they serve a vital role beyond simply lifting us out of our often dreary lives. Delving into places and experiences different from our own expands our understanding of the world, broadens our imaginations, and deepens our empathy.

And when the world around us gets a little too real, it helps keep us sane. 2020 was a challenging year for us all, filled with stress, uncertainty, lost dreams, and tragedy. But even when we were stuck at home, our minds could escape into books and other entertainments for a respite from the new and difficult reality we'd been thrust into.

When the lockdowns began in March and the year started to look grim, I asked my writer friends and colleagues to contribute a short story for an anthology project aimed at providing some escape. Big adventure, small adventure—they could create whatever sort of story they liked, so long as it took readers on a daring quest or fantastic journey into strange new worlds. I am pleased to present the fruits of their hard work in this book.

It was a pleasure working with all the contributors —the amount of talent and imagination they provided was amazing. And I want to give a special nod to Susan

Conner for being an additional pair of editing eyes when I needed them. Thank you, Susan!

Without further ado, please enjoy this collection of adventure stories. May they offer you a small measure of escape when times get tough.

THE FAMILIAR

MELION TRAVERSE

Thaddeus felt terrible that he caused the sorcerer duel. Oh, Ara told him it wasn't his fault. Not *really* his fault, she'd explained, but he had been the one whom the town sorcerer's hawk had attacked. And the hawk had attacked him because he wasn't being careful. If Thaddeus should have known one thing, it was that a stoat must live with caution as a watchword, but he'd felt safe in Ara's garden.

He'd been snuffling after a delicious vole on the edge of the garden and had just set to digging his way down into its tunnel when the hawk plunged from the sky.

Instinct and something in the corner of his eye alerted Thaddeus, who dove aside and dashed into the cabbage just as a talon scraped his fur. Primal terror and the dark memory that was all too similar sent him bolting through the garden with his eyes set on the cottage door.

The wooden door swung open, and Ara stood at the threshold with a broom in her hand and fury that could have burnished bronze aglow on her face. She had seen the hawk swoop down on Thaddeus. He dashed past her ankles and scuttled into the space behind the stove.

When he peeked his head out, it was in time to see the door slam shut as Ara marched out of the cottage, propelled by her blazing anger.

Thaddeus scampered across the floor and jumped up to his window perch. Ara turned down the path and vanished into the forest.

By the time he managed the window latch and dashed off in pursuit, it was too late. Thaddeus arrived in a wide forest glade to find trees streaked with scorches and burnt leaves drifting like dirty snow. The trees swallowed the silhouette of the town sorcerer with a hawk perched upon his arm. The air reeked of magical fire, and when Ara scooped Thaddeus up and pressed him against her, he felt the unnatural heat lingering in her fingers.

"I lost, Thad," she whispered in a voice that shook as badly as her trembling body. "I lost, and he said he'd never teach somebody like me—somebody without control." Then she carried Thaddeus back home as the little stoat tried to nuzzle away her tears.

* * *

Thaddeus cursed the lamentable shortness of his legs. While it only made sense that he should have tiny legs on account of possessing a tiny body, Thaddeus's appendages were not conducive to scuttling about a town filled with shuffling boots and stomping hooves. He wove his sinuous body through the ankles of countless people, snaking over feet as he scurried along the raised sidewalk. Drying blood crusted on one of his shoulders from where a rock had ricocheted off the cobblestones and caught him a sharp, glancing blow that cut into his fur.

But Ara needed help, and she was worth risking a little blood and the hazards of an unforgiving town. Here and there a person yelped and swung a booted foot his direction as he darted past, thinking him one of the countless vermin that scrounged the town's garbage piles, but Thaddeus was no common vermin. No, indeed. Thaddeus might have been a stoat, but he was also the familiar to one of the greatest sorcerers the little town could hope to produce. Or at least, in his view, his master *would* be one of the greatest sorcerers if she survived.

At the moment, her survival teetered on a sharp precipice, and much depended upon Thaddeus and his tiny limbs. He scampered up onto a barrel, surveying the cobblestone street for his next move as he gave himself a chance to pause. But he couldn't pause for long, not when Ara depended upon him. *I've got this, Ara*, he promised. His promise had become like an incantation repeated again and again until it wore a groove into his brain. Thaddeus could not give up, not when his master lay dying of a strange fever. A magical fever brought on by the sorcerer's duel two days ago.

Why, Ara? Thaddeus thought. He jumped down from the barrel with a sigh and made a calculated dash alongside a building, pressed against the rough boards of the wall as he dodged feet. But he knew why: about the only thing that matched Ara's affection for Thaddeus was her temper. Thaddeus was no ordinary stoat, and that had been no ordinary hawk. A familiar, just like him. Well . . . if he was being honest—and Thaddeus *did* try to be an honest stoat—the hawk wasn't just like him. It was more powerful, as its master was more powerful.

Thaddeus knew Ara would one day be a great sorcerer, but that day wasn't yet here. She had many books to consume down to their spines and scrolls to study in great gulps of knowledge before she reached her potential. Today, Ara was a girl with power roiling in her limbs, burning through her muscles and devouring her bones with the need to be released. Now she lay in the grip of a magical fever with only her faithful familiar to seek out the cure.

And the only place to find the ingredient Ara would need was in the home of the sorcerer who had dueled against her.

The town sorcerer made his home outside the walls of the mayoral estate set within the beating heart of the settlement. Thaddeus wove among the press of people until he reached the garden gate of the sorcerer's home. Getting past the gate was no trouble for a stoat who could simply slip amid the thick ivy vines and scale the walls. A rat darted along the wall tops, and Thaddeus gave a chuckling hiss that sent the rodent bounding the other direction. Every rat knew in the primal parts of their brain that stoats were predators to be avoided.

Cats on the other hand . . . The stoat snorted in frustration as he spotted the orange cat lazing in a sun patch like a mottled spoonful of marmalade. Tail swishing, the feline drifted in that state between dozing and awareness in the garden. Thaddeus would never be able to slip past unnoticed. Thaddeus twitched his nose in thought, casually scenting the air as he studied the scene about him. One window was open with a curtain

ruffling in the breeze; he could easily get through that
window if the cat weren't watching. But the cat lay in
the center of the garden, a dash of ginger speckled
amid the grass. The other entrance was possibly the
backdoor where the door didn't reach the threshold,
leaving a narrow gap through which the stoat could
flatten himself and scoot through. His eyes darted
again to the cat as it flicked the tip of its tail.

    No, thought Thaddeus. *It'll be on me in a heartbeat
if I get stuck going under the door.* A shiver rippled
over his long body at the thought of being pinned
beneath the door as the cat pounced upon him exposed
and defenseless. That would be just as bad as the hawk.
Worse, perhaps. Not counting the tail, the cat wasn't
larger than some rabbits Thaddeus had hunted, but
rabbits didn't have fangs and claws and the inborn joy
of watching a smaller creature suffer.

    Flattening himself beneath the vines, Thaddeus
scurried along the wall top, surveying the perimeter of
the garden. The front door fit tightly against the
threshold, and no other windows were open. He
paused briefly to consider a crack in the wall. Maybe he
could squeeze through there. No telling where it would
lead, but it might lead to an opportunity. Or it might
lead nowhere, and he'd be stuck in the wall as the cat
paced back and forth, waiting for the moment
desperation made the stoat bold.

    Thaddeus doubled back to find the cat still
stretched in the puddle of late afternoon sun, licking
one of its paws. But now he saw that a window on the
second story was open. Even better. He could be up the
wall of the house and through the window in the twitch
of a whisker. Except he first had to reach the house. He

thought about just abandoning caution and making a wild leap, hoping to grasp hold of the vines that twined around the trellis like lacework. *Don't be a fool, Thaddeus,* he admonished. He couldn't make such a jump, and his failure would mean Ara didn't get her ingredient.

Thinking of Ara, Thaddeus hunched on the wall top and flicked his tail, sparing a glance to the sky in search of hawks. She had looked terrible when he'd darted from the house that day. Lips parched, red eyes sunk into dark caverns, she could barely hold her cup of water. And little Thaddeus had sat atop her blanket with nothing he could do but nudge her fever-warmed cheek with his damp nose. He had tried to cheer her with the antics she found so laughable, but even his frenzied war dance which had always delighted her as he jumped and rolled with dramatic vigor had only coaxed a distracted sort of smile in response.

The day before, she had smoothed a scroll across her lap, the parchment rustling in her unsteady hands, and read the ingredients needed to cure a fever brought on by magic drain. Simple enough, she had told him. Except for one ingredient: dried and powdered lizard tongue. At the mention of the ingredient, Thaddeus had wrinkled his nose, but Ara laughed weakly and ran her fingertips over his glossy head.

"Not from real lizards, of course," she had said, trailing her fingers to scratch under his chin. "Lizard tongue is a rare flower. I could find it, but drying it takes work and it takes time. And I'm afraid I don't have time, Thaddeus." She had then gone to bed and not gotten back out. Thaddeus had run to the little leather satchel on Ara's bedside and pulled out a gold coin, the engraving of some human's face worn down to an echo more than an image by the countless fingers which had traded it. He could take the coin and run to the herbalist's shop. Certainly he'd been there often enough as he perched upon Ara's shoulder with his tail draped across her neck. But Ara had only shook her head. "No, my friend. Lizard tongue is of no use to non-sorcerers, and Hera would have no reason to keep it."

Thaddeus had put the coin back into the pouch, and curled himself up on Ara's pillow, but he'd not gone to sleep because her words ran through his mind like fleeing hares. Non-sorcerers would not need such a plant, but what about the other sorcerer? Thaddeus knew where he lived because Ara had pointed out the house before—many times before—when they had strolled through the lively town streets. Each time she would poke a drowsing Thaddeus to wakefulness and say, "See? That's where the town sorcerer lives. A real sorcerer, Thaddeus, and I'll study magic from him someday. Even if he doesn't take students, I swear I will."

If any house would have dried lizard tongue, it would be the house of a powerful sorcerer. And he must be a powerful sorcerer, indeed, to have so handily bested Ara in a duel. Certainly Thaddeus would find what he sought in that house, if only he could get past the cat.

Another rat appeared amid the vines, head popping up over the edge of the fence. Here was Thaddeus's chance. With a sharp hiss and a snap of his teeth, Thaddeus lunged toward the rat. For a heartbeat, the

rodent froze, fur puffed out in terror, but with
Thaddeus aiming toward him, the rat jolted into
motion and spun about. The rodent gave a squeak of
fear and darted down the vines with Thaddeus in
pursuit. The stone wall offered excellent purchase, and
the stoat descended so quickly that he had to pull
himself back from catching his quarry. He needed the
rat to run.

The rat careened through the garden in the last
golden glow of sunlight. At once, the cat came to
wakefulness, leaping from its lazing posture of repose
into the muscle-taut crouch of a hunting beast. On ran
the rat, and the cat bounded after it, ears alert and tail
twitching.

Thaddeus seized his chance and launched himself
across the garden, whipping through neatly-tended
herbs and dashing across the grass as he ran for the
house. The rat bolted toward the door, and there the
cat seized its prey, batting the rodent for sport.
Engaged with its new toy, the cat gave Thaddeus no
mind as the stoat reached the house and grasped hold
of the rough stones. He climbed and climbed even as
his injured shoulder pained him and fresh blood
trickled free. If the cat lost interest in the rat, it could
turn around with a bounding leap and be upon him in
a moment. Heart slamming in his throat, Thaddeus
reached the window ledge on the second story and
dove inside without a backward glance or a pause to
look about.

Panting, Thaddeus huddled in the shadow that fell
below the window and darted his eyes about the room.
The tangy scent of herbs and flowers flooded the space
from corner to crevasse, and a mess of scrolls and

books spilled across the floor as though a bookshelf had been tossed from the wall. It was how Thaddeus imagined Ara's room looking if he were to cast his mind into the future. A single lamp glowed at a desk, its light illuminating a large shelf crammed with bottles, all of them painstakingly labeled.

The cat might be amusing itself outside, but the sorcerer could be lurking anywhere. Thaddeus ducked from book stack to scroll pile as he crossed the room. Up he leapt onto the chair and from there to the desk. He spied an inkwell filled to the brim, and for a spiteful moment, Thaddeus had a desire to knock the ink all over the parchment spread on the desk, and then run-roll all through it. It would serve the sorcerer right for hurting Ara.

But it won't help, will it? the stoat thought as he crouched beside the inkwell, one paw raised to send it spilling across the desk. No, his one task was to find the powdered lizard tongue, and he had wasted enough time on account of the cat.

Sitting back on his haunches, Thaddeus tilted his head to survey the rows upon rows of bottles. An ordinary stoat would be at a complete loss, but Thaddeus gave his tail a twitch of pride that he was not ordinary. Every sorcerer worthy of the title taught their familiar to read. That was what Ara had told him when she first set down a scroll filled with letters before him. She had awakened him from the narrow world of being just a stoat after she found him lying injured from the attack of a different hawk. *Always hawks*, Thaddeus thought bitterly. He remembered her mingled delight and pity at seeing him lying with heaving flanks amid

the flower garden. Pity at his poor condition and
delight that surely he was meant to be her familiar.

Of course, Thaddeus hadn't known such things at
the time. All he had known was fear and pain, and then
a human hand reaching for him. But the human made
sounds that chased the fear from his brain, so he didn't
bite as she gently scooped him into her hands.

And it felt nice to have a human petting him and
offering him choice nibbles of food after she had
cleaned his injuries, and all the while the magic wove
itself unseen upon his mind. Before Thaddeus even
realized, his world had shifted from what it was, to
what it forevermore would be. He brought her
laughter, and she brought him knowledge. And he
found one night, after he had used his little claws to
knead her pillow into just the right shape for him to lay
down upon beside her head, that they brought each
other comfort and happiness.

So if Ara needed him to start knocking about
through bottles on a dangerous sorcerer's shelves in
order to save her life, well, he'd do it without
hesitation.

Thaddeus hopped onto the shelf and started
reading. It was, of course, too much to ask that a
sorcerer properly alphabetize a jumble of ingredients.
*Firethistle. Wolf's paw. Ghost shadow. Shimmering
water parsley.* Thaddeus hadn't the first idea what one
did with any of the ingredients, except sneeze as he
knocked one over. At last he climbed to a shelf and
found a little green bottle that read: *Lizard tongue,
dried and powdered.* His paw reached for the bottle,
and he wondered how he would get it from the shelf

and out of the room, when the world filled with the wild beating of wings.

Wings and talons. Everything was violent motion and Thaddeus jumped from the shelf, scattering bottles across the desk and floor. Clutching the green bottle under one arm, the stoat bounced from the table and onto the floor, crying out as he landed on his injured shoulder. Overhead, a white hawk with grey bars across its breast flew through the room, screeching a hunting cry. It was the hawk who had almost seized Thaddeus as a snack two days before in Ara's garden.

The window was open, and Thaddeus could make his escape, but he couldn't move quickly while holding the bottle. And he couldn't leave his prize, not when he thought of Ara lying in bed growing weaker and weaker as the fever burned through her like fire gnawing a forest.

Whipping his body around, Thaddeus smacked his tail into a bottle, sending the container into the air with force. It thudded against the hawk, startling the bird in mid-attack and causing it to turn aside. Grasping the bottle of lizard tongue, Thaddeus dragged the precious ingredient across the floor as fast as his body would allow, scooting desperately backwards toward the window. Stacks of books toppled as Thaddeus fumbled about. Scraps of loose paper swirled. Thaddeus rolled the bottle beneath a chair and dove after it.

Still calling loudly, the hawk landed on the chair back. Waiting. Shivers rippled down Thaddeus's sleek body. His body remembered the burning pain of talons from all those months ago. He clutched the bottle to himself and shrank down as small as he could, desperate to stay away from the edges of the chair that sheltered him. Any moment the hawk would jump to the floor and begin snapping at him with its beak. Thaddeus knew that would be his end. He had survived one hawk just to be eaten by another.

It wouldn't be just his end, but Ara's too.

"Hey now, Aquila, what in the name of the hundred hells is happening in here?" a voice rumbled as a man's heavy boots stomped into the room. The sorcerer.

Thaddeus turned to the window. Escape was so close . . . Without the bottle, he could be through it and down into the evening shadows and freedom. But he couldn't leave the bottle. Thaddeus gripped the bottle tighter and cursed the hawk with every unpleasant word Ara had ever taught him.

A hand grasped Thaddeus by the scruff. He squeaked as he found himself hauled into the air, the bottle clattering to the ground. Hissing, he twisted about to come face to face with the sorcerer. Thaddeus swiped with his claws at the man's face, but the sorcerer laughed and pulled his head away. "Oh now, aren't you the little fighter." The sorcerer looked down where the green bottle had rolled against the wall. Still keeping a hold of Thaddeus, he picked up the bottle. "Ah, lizard tongue, is it? That's where I've seen you— you're the young sorcerer's familiar, are you not?"

Thaddeus hissed again, but surprise took the edge off the stoat's threat. He had not expected the tone of pity in the sorcerer's voice. Anger, mockery, fury. Any of those he expected, but not something that sounded like the pain in Thaddeus's own heart when he thought about Ara.

"Foolish child," the man said, holding up the bottle and looking through it as though great mysteries lay within the colored glass. "But all of us sorcerers are young and foolish at some point, aren't we now?" He set Thaddeus down on the desk and waved back the hawk with a sharp motion from his hand and a warning to behave himself.

What do I do? Thaddeus gathered himself to launch his little body at the sorcerer's face. He had, after all, been the cause of Ara's sickness. But the sorcerer seemed little concerned with the stoat as he popped open the bottle of powdered lizard's tongue.

"Drained the magic right out of herself with that fire spell, didn't she?" the sorcerer continued, tapping out some of the powder onto a square of parchment he'd torn from a page. "Stupid pup, trying a spell like that without proper wards. *Hmph*, not that I should be surprised. Nearly fried my own skin right off my skeleton with a lightning spell when I was her age. Maybe she'll learn to use her brain before her magic from now on," he continued, clearly not talking to Thaddeus who still sat on his back legs and watched as the sorcerer used a snip of twine to tie the parchment into a bundle. "Here then, little weasel—oh, no, I guess you're a stoat, aren't you? She doesn't like when you're called a weasel, does she? Take this back to her straight away. I'd bring it, but this is one of those things young sorcerers need to do for themselves—it's how we learn to stop being stupid pups. But I'll come by tomorrow evening and check on her."

The sorcerer thrust the bundle of measured herbs into Thaddeus's paws. The stoat glanced out the window where the twilight gloom gathered. Somewhere in the coalescing shadows, the cat still waited. And owls soon, too, Thaddeus thought with a shudder.

"Hmm, it seems to me that sending a stoat out into the dangers of the evening would be a poor way to see that your sorcerer receives her ingredient," the man added, rubbing his angular face as he studied Thaddeus. The sorcerer turned to where the hawk sat upon a perch, preening itself. "Very well. Aquila, you've made quite the mess in here. Transport this stoat back home while I clean up all of this." He made an emphatic sweeping gesture to the whirlwind of parchment across the room.

Thaddeus looked at the hawk's talons and froze in primal terror. He remembered that day when he dragged himself into Ara's garden. It was a different hawk, smaller, dusty brown, but the pain of the talons slicing into Thaddeus's skin as he dodged aside still burned. The stoat gripped the pouch of lizard tongue closer, but inched away from Aquila. After all, Aquila would have feasted upon him just as readily as a regular hawk the other day.

"You're a brave little creature, but you must be braver still if you want to help your sorcerer in time," the man said. "If you're her familiar, you will find yourself in many dangerous places, because the life of a sorcerer isn't what she probably thinks it is—it's not how any of us think it is until we're engulfed in it. But if you want her to live, you must defy your instincts. I promise that Aquila won't hurt you."

Ara, Thaddeus thought, seeing her lying in bed. If he waited too long, would she be able to mix the ingredients into the cure she needed? He swallowed down the sour fear and edged closer to the hawk.

"It says much of your sorcerer that she inspires such courage in her familiar," said the man. Thaddeus shook from nose to tail tip as the hawk's talons wrapped around his lithe form, but he stifled the squeak of fear gathering in his throat. "Very well. I will offer your impetuous friend the training she's hounded me for. Now get going so that I will have a student left to teach."

With a powerful beat of wings and a leap, Aquila launched them out the window and into the deepening evening. Thaddeus's stomach plunged at the sensation of climbing into the air with nothing but hawk talons holding him aloft. But Ara needed him, and so he clutched the parcel of powdered flower, and stared into the distance. Any resident who happened to glance at the moon that evening would think a hawk had caught a tasty weasel for its meal, but they couldn't know the truth of it. They couldn't know that it was no ordinary animal held in the talons of the hawk. Nobody who witnessed them fly overhead would know that Thaddeus was the familiar to a girl who would become the most powerful sorcerer that town had ever seen. One day, that is, after she had studied.

Melion Traverse lives with one spouse, two dogs, and an acceptable amount of chaos. Melion has had works appear in *Cast of Wonders, Cosmic Roots and Eldritch Shores*, and *Deep Magic*, among other publications. Melion's debut YA sword and sorcery novel, *Exile*, has been published by Authors 4 Authors Publishing. When not writing, Melion practices historical fencing, trains in Brazilian Jiu-Jitsu, lifts weights, reads Latin, and wages the eternal Battle of the Dog Fur.

GARDEN MAGIC

K D KELLEY

In a countryside of green, rolling hills, where crops and sheep were found in abundance and not much of anything else, a village spread across a hill like a luck-veil over a pregnant woman's belly. The village went by the original name of Hillcrest, and in this village lived a greenwitch.

Not in the town proper, of course. The greenwitch required space for her gardens and there was little of that to be had on the hill. The villagers required the peace of their homes and minds, and there was little of that to be had near the home of a greenwitch. A place where magic grew wild until it was tamed into charms, spells, and potions.

So the greenwitch's cottage sat at the base of the hill where a bit of the town had spread like a dollop of melted frosting off a warm cake. The mill and blacksmith sat between the cottage and town, and it was from the miller's doorstep that a group of children contemplated the witch's cottage beyond the blacksmith's yard.

"My brother says she's lived more than ten lifetimes and makes blood sacrifices so she doesn't die."

Elend stood apart from the others, half-listening to Claren's claims which grew more outlandish with each telling. In Elend's considered opinion, with the weight of his fourteen years behind it, Claren was a 'stupid sort'. Loud and brash with more attitude than brains.

Unfortunately, at sixteen, Claren was also a handsome and accomplished sort of boy, not to mention from a rich family, which balanced out the stupid enough that other children were drawn to him. He was also the sort to punch and kick anyone who dared draw attention to his flaws.

Elend had no particular desire to be kicked or punched on that afternoon, so the other half of his attention was plotting how to slip away with the bag of flour his gran had sent him after. Preferably without being noticed by Claren or his two lackeys.

Claren was making a mighty effort to impress the cluster of four girls with his knowledge and wouldn't be above taunting Elend if it raised his esteem in the girls' eyes.

Of the girls, two were enraptured by Claren's stories; a set of twins with only one mind between them (another of Elend's considered opinions). The other two were sisters as well, though seven years separated that pair. And each had more sense than any of the other five in the group. Sarai, the elder, was frowning with disapproval. Minea, the younger, frowned also, but in confusion.

"But then why does she look old?" Minea asked. "If she could work that magic, why wouldn't she make herself young and pretty?"

Claren's smug expression slipped briefly into uncertainty before setting into annoyance. "Because that would be suspicious," he scoffed, "obviously."

The answer did nothing to clear Minea's confusion. "Why?"

"She's a witch, that's why. Everyone would know she uses her dark arts to fool them."

"Witches can't be young and pretty?" Minea pressed. "Do they only get magic when they're old? And if everyone already knows she's a witch, then how does she fool them? And if they're not fooled, then why doesn't she just make herself young and pretty?"

"That's right," Claren said, though no one seemed to know what question he was answering, his lips twisting in a mean sneer. "After years and years of sacrificing little girls and eating their hearts."

Minea shrank back against her sister. Elend felt his stomach twist, two sides wrestling against one another. The unfamiliar desire to stand up to Claren and the all too familiar respect for Claren's fists.

Sarai had no such misgivings, possibly because she knew Claren wouldn't hit her, and more likely because she was made of stronger stuff. Elend sighed in relief and blushed in shame when she put herself between Claren and Minea.

"That's not true, stop scaring her," she challenged, crossing her arms. "I don't think your brother knows what he's talking about. If he really said anything at all. Let's go home, Minea."

"Oh, he knows," Claren said, stepping into their path. He glanced at his lackeys who were looking at their shoes, and the adoring twins who weren't quite so adoring anymore.

"Really?" Sarai's voice dripped sarcasm like hot wax from a lit candle. "He knows more than the mayor and everyone else in town does he? And how is it your brother is so very special?"

She stepped into him, pointing a finger under his nose. A gesture that had Elend applauding her bravery and nervously clutching his wheat sack closer to his chest.

"I'll have you know she brought an apple pie when Mama was sick last winter. She said she baked a wish for wellness into it."

"Ha!" Claren pointed a finger right back. "You see? She spelled you."

"It was delicious and my ma got better the next day. The witch didn't charge us anything. Not coins or blood or hearts."

Minea poked her head around her sister, her chin jutting out. She stomped her foot. "I think she's nice."

"So do I." Sarai took the little girl's hand and stepped around the older boy.

Claren turned to follow, searching for a way to redeem himself, and hit upon a better victim: Elend, who had unfortunately chosen that moment to slip away behind Sarai.

"What's your hurry, Elend? Need to get back to your master?" Claren covered his mouth in mock embarrassment. "Oh that's right, you don't have a master."

Elend dropped his head, feeling his face flush at the insult. He should have long since been apprenticed, but no respectable tradesman would have him. No matter how well they thought of his gran, they thought less of his parents. Gran told him over and over not to worry, but Elend knew that without a trade he would never be anything but a burden to her.

He mumbled an excuse and walked away, humiliated.

Claren strode over, blocking Elend's escape. "Stay and tell us what you think of the witch. It's not like you have anything else to do."

Elend found himself the center of attention. Morbid enjoyment radiated from the boys and twins who anticipated a fight, while Sarai and Minea clutched hands and looked on fearfully.

It stung his pride that Sarai could stand up to Claren herself, but be afraid for him. It was enough to goad him into standing straight, though he still had to look up to meet the older boy's eyes.

"My gran says the greenwitch is a good person and no one to be afraid of." Flushed with the success of getting the words out clearly, if not at full volume, he added, "Sarai is right, your brother is a liar."

"Oh-ho! Well then, since she and your gran are such good friends, maybe you should get us some of those apples."

Elend stepped back at this unexpected turn, his courage failing him. "No."

"Why not? If she's so kind, she won't mind giving up a couple apples to some hungry kids, right?"

His followers nodded in fascinated agreement, eyes sparkling with excitement at the dare. Claren grinned, bolstered by the support.

Elend didn't find anything exciting about filching from the greenwitch's garden, even if it might make him look brave and adventurous to Sarai.

"Not me. I-I have to get home with Gran's flour."

Elend started for the village, shoulders tight, awaiting certain doom in the form of Claren's fists. When it came, it was worse.

"Run away, coward, just like your sheep-dung father."

Elend stumbled as if Claren had thrown the punch he expected. Out of breath and trembling, he said, "What did you say?"

"Everyone knows the coward ran away instead of marrying your ma."

Elend whirled, so hot he thought he'd turn to a pillar of fire. His mouth opened but the words burnt to ash before he could speak them. Claren smiled, but his eyes were glittering and angry.

"Tell me, did your ma die of shame, or was it to escape raising a bastard?"

The flour sack thudded to the ground in a puff of dirt. "Don't you talk about my ma."

Elend couldn't feel his legs but somehow Claren's ugly, smirking face got closer and Elend clenched his hands into fists.

Sarai pushed between them, dragging Minea along with her. "Elend, can you walk home with us? My ma has something to send to your gran."

It wasn't her shaking voice or trembling hand on his shoulder that stopped him, it was Minea, her wide eyes full of tears. A reaction not even Claren had caused.

He took her hand. "Let's go."

"Go on then." Claren made clucking noises. "Hide behind the little girl's skirts. She'll protect you."

Elend nudged the flour bag with his foot. "I'm not scared of him or the greenwitch," he muttered.

"I know," Sarai said, but she wouldn't look at him.

Claren was still clucking and laughing.

Elend pressed his lips together. This time the angry flash didn't burn his throat or haze his vision or cloud his mind. He knew his purpose with crystal clarity.

"You want an apple? I'll get you an apple."

He left the flour in the road and didn't bother stopping to confront Claren, just clipped his shoulder as he passed. He ignored the jeers from the boys, the squeals from the girls, and especially ignored Sarai yelling for him to stop.

He had a mission. A quest to wipe the smirk from Claren's face, the pity from Sarai's, and to see that no one, ever, insulted his ma or compared him to his lying, coward father again.

He had an apple to steal.

* * *

The garden gate was just a garden gate. Whitewashed slats a little taller than Elend that he could peek over if he lifted to his toes. He didn't. The fence was also just a fence. More slats that ended at the house in one direction, disappeared into a thick hedge in the other.

Elend reached for the gate latch, then pulled back. Glanced over his shoulder. They were all still there: Claren and his lackeys, the twins, Minea, Sarai. Standing in the middle of the road now, watching. If they hadn't been, Elend could have slipped away, hidden at home, told them later that he tried and the greenwitch kicked him out. But they all watched him now.

Sarai shook her head, telling him to stop, her eyes wide.

Elend gritted his teeth and faced the gate once more. Maybe she *would* kick him out, in front of all of them, proof that he'd tried. That he was no coward.

He took a deep breath and touched the latch with a finger.

Nothing happened.

He put his hand on it.

Nothing.

He turned it, and still nothing happened. The gate was just a gate, the latch just a latch. It moved easily and the gate swung open.

He flinched, turning with one shoulder raised, certain he would be attacked by a slap of magic, or a dragon, or an enchanted garden gnome. Something.

Beyond the gate spread a garden: plots of flowers, herbs, and vegetables in neat beds with gravel rows between, draped by a soft haze of pollen and the warming afternoon. Birds flew by, bees buzzed. Tiny rose bushes lined the path leading away from the gate. And, when he leaned in beyond the gate, Elend could see a pair of apple trees at the far end. Not that far at all.

It was a comforting sort of place, a place that could wash away worries and soothe fears like a lullaby after a bad dream. Elend felt calm and peaceful as the garden drew him in, welcomed him as if he belonged, as if it only waited for him to come home.

The gate slammed shut behind him, shocking him out of the warm daze.

It was locked, the latch frozen. It wouldn't move, nor did the gate, though he pounded and pounded on the slats. Not even a rattle. He turned and put his back to it, heaving in great gulps of air to slow his racing heart.

Just stuck, he told himself, rusty and old.

Since the gate wouldn't open, there was no way out but through. That was what Gran would say. 'Elend,' she'd tell him, 'when you hit a problem that blocks your way, there's no going back. The only way out is through'.

The trees weren't far, and he knew the greenwitch's property ran to the stream. Get an apple, get to the stream, wade or swim his way out.

Solid plan. Elend pushed off the gate and started down the path.

The first attack was nothing more than a tug on his pant leg. The next stung his hand. Looking down at the thin cut, oozing blood, he didn't see what then whipped his rear; smart and stinging like the willow switch Gran kept in the corner as a reminder for good behavior. Startled, he froze instead of whirling around, and saw the next attack. A branch from a tiny rose bush, longer and more supple than it should have been, struck his arm, leaving behind a tear in his shirt.

Discovered, they made no more stealthy attempts. Branches came at him from every direction, sharp whips scraping exposed skin and ripping fabric. Elend ran, covering his face with his arms, until he was clear of the bushes.

"Ha!" he crowed, safely out of their reach. His gran would have fits over all the extra darning, and he'd lost a bit of skin, but he'd come out victorious.

A straight path was now in front of him, cutting the garden in half, and leading to the apple trees. He set off, sure of a quick and easy success. Even if he did eye the plants lining the path, alert now to the type of attack he could expect.

Elend didn't look up. And he should have looked up.

A bee landed on his shoulder. Elend knew slapping or swatting would only end up making it mad, so he gently brushed it off. It hovered in front of his face, buzzing angrily, so he moved to the side and around it. Another buzzed in his ear, or maybe it was the same one. Elend jerked his head to the side and kept walking. Two more appeared, one that dove in and popped against his forehead before going off in a wobbling flight, another that tickled the side of his neck. Then three more, then more, and more, until Elend found himself in the middle of a buzzing cloud.

"Don't swat, don't swat," he chanted, and dropped to the ground to crawl out of the swarm.

It followed him down and he crawled faster, ducking and swerving until he was out of the cloud, then jumped back to his feet to run again. A new swarm swooped down in front of him and he skidded to run down a different path. The original bunch flew behind, buzzing so loud he could feel the air vibrate against his neck, forcing him to keep going forward. New swarms cropped up, forcing him to change directions until he couldn't remember where he'd come from, didn't know where he was going. More paths than he'd seen in the garden, more than the space of the garden could possibly hold.

He raced by two more gravel lanes before he realized no new bees came to harry him, and the ones herding him were gone. He bent over, hands to his knees, panting and examining his body. All those bees, all that running, and not a single sting. Feeling accomplished, and more than a little lucky, he straightened to look for the apple trees to get his bearings.

What he found was miles and miles of garden beds, at least that's how it appeared to Elend's frightened mind. No longer neat plots divided by straight paths, these were overgrown plantings, tangling one into another. The paths—what there were of them—were narrow grass walks, though some were so studded with rocks it could have been cobblestone. And not one of them was straight.

Some of the beds overflowed onto the paths in graceful sweeps like a rich lady's gown. Some of them had plants so tall they shaded the paths. Some arched over them in natural trellises.

So this, Elend thought, was how the greenwitch's garden really looked. Wild and magical. All those neat and tidy rows were an illusion, some enchantment designed to hide its true appearance from wandering eyes.

And the apple trees were now nowhere in sight.

"They're hidden," he reassured himself. Just hidden by all these tall plants. Once he found his way back to the main path, he'd be fine. Straight shot to the trees.

With a decisive nod and all the illusory assurance of a lost wanderer convinced they weren't lost at all, Elend began to walk. South, he was sure, had been the direction to the trees. The first turn he'd taken running away from the bees, he was positive, had been to the right and he hadn't run back across.

"West, I need to go west."

Elend squinted at the sun, adjusted his direction at the first available path, and kept walking.

Something whispered behind him.

He whirled around with fists raised—to hit or defend, he wasn't sure, only that he wouldn't be caught by a surprise attack again. But the path was empty. Only tall bushes with slender branches swaying in a breeze against each other. But none of the other plants, or the grass on the path, moved. No cooling wind brushed his cheeks or ruffled his hair.

Swish. Swish.

"Nothing to worry about," Elend said nervously, hastening on his way. "Nothing at all. Just a garden. Just an empty old garden."

He continued to talk to himself, to fill the space with more than himself and the plants. To ward off the eerie prickling that was trying to crawl up his back like the tickling of those bees.

"Any minute now I'll find the main path again and the trees. I'll pick the apple and shove it in Claren's face." Yeah, that's what he'd do.

He ignored the whispering behind him, to his left.

"Or," he mused, "I could give it to Sarai. Present it to her with a deep bow and lots of hand twirling like the Mayor did when Lord Belton visited. She'd like that, I bet."

There might have been a snicker on the tail end of the latest whisper, but gone so quick he wasn't sure. He frowned and picked up his pace.

"I'm not running," he told the garden in general, "but I have to get back before they go home. Otherwise Claren will say I bought it at the market."

Claren, Claren, the swishing whispers seemed to
tease.

Elend moved his legs in a very fast walk. "I'm not
running. I'm not running."

The grassy path he was not running on veered to
the right in a sharp curve. Before he could follow, a
pink flower popped up in his face. As big as his head, it
had three spindly stamens that seemed to smile at him.

"Hello," it said with a puff of white glitter.

Elend screamed. Then ran, watching the pink
bloom over his shoulder as it bobbed with his—her?—
fellows on stems, waving in very un-flowerlike
behavior.

Looking behind as he was, he ran shoulder first into
a door—his head knocking into it a fraction later. He
stumbled away, rubbing at both places sure to bruise,
and hit against another door, the knob digging into his
side.

"Hey! Ouch!"

Elend was surrounded by four walls much taller
than his head; two with doors, two of stacked stones.
The floor was smooth paving under his feet and there
was no ceiling.

Elend swallowed nervously. This room was no
simple illusion or enchantment, but real and solid—his
sore head attested to that. If the garden could
randomly change its appearance, and create rooms on
a whim, how would he ever find his way out?

"I hope you don't expect a door to apologize,"
chirped a tiny voice. "You seem like a smart enough
boy to know doors don't talk."

"Of course I know doors don't talk," Elend snapped,
annoyed out of his fear and relieved at hearing another

person speaking. "Where are you?" he asked as he was alone in the open room.

"Oh dear, oh dear, maybe not so smart. Up here, dear."

The top of each wall was lined with flower boxes, full of yellow daisies. An especially large bloom with a deep brown center looked down on him. Doors didn't talk but apparently flowers did in a witch's garden.

"Hello?"

The large daisy swiveled its head one way then the other. "Do you hear that, dears? So polite." The other daisies tittered and nodded to one another. "Well, smart, polite, boy, which will you choose?"

"Which what?"

"Oh dear, oh dear, why do they never understand? Choose a door, dear, it's the only way out."

Well of course it was, Elend thought grumpily, though he carefully kept it to himself. He examined both doors, taking only three steps in each direction. It was a very small space.

On the door he'd run into, was a picture of a house that looked much like his own. The other held the image of two trees. Even a dunce could figure it out. One led home, the other to the apples.

"Maybe I should climb over the wall instead," Elend said. The choices seemed awfully simple and anything might be waiting for him beyond the doors in a magic garden.

"I wouldn't do that if I were you."

The flowers shook as if blown by a gust of wind. Petals rained down on Elend and he shivered at the warning tone of the daisy.

"Why not?"

"No one likes a cheat, dear. The garden seems to like you, it doesn't allow just anyone beyond the gate, you know. Best not to anger it."

If the garden used attacking roses and swarming bees when it liked someone, he didn't want to find out what happened if he made it mad. One of the doors it was then. His hand was on the apple tree door when the large daisy tsked.

"Are you sure, dear?"

"I am."

It tilted its head, which was more of a spin, like a pinwheel. "Why?"

"Because if I get an apple, Claren will stop pushing me around."

And Elend was tired of being pushed around. Tired of Sarai thinking he was a coward. Tired of everyone believing he'd turn out just like his father, that his mother had died of shame because of him.

"Everything will be better if I get that apple. No one will call me a coward then."

"And is that so very important, dear? What other people think?"

"Yes. It is. People don't pick on someone brave enough to get a greenwitch's apple. Some people might even want that boy for an apprentice," he said quietly, then squinted up at the daisy. "This garden is magic, right?"

"I think that would be obvious by now, dear."

"And if I pick this door," he pointed to the house, "I'll go home. But the other door will take me to the trees, right?"

"That's right." Its tone was very patient, like a teacher encouraging a small child reciting the alphabet.

"If the garden is letting me choose, it must be all right if I get an apple," he said with a nod and the twisted logic of those determined to be right.

He opened the apple tree door.

"I wouldn't say that, dear," the daisy said. "Maybe the garden wants to let you go home."

Too late, Elend was through the door, leaving behind the daisies shaking their petals and calling, "Oh dear, oh dear."

The wild garden was gone, and Elend found himself on a smooth, paved path lined with neatly-trimmed box hedges. They were short, just about shoulder high, and he could see two apple trees in the distance. The path led straight forward, but there was a T where it joined another not far off, so Elend went to it and turned toward the trees. Straight down to a dead end. He hadn't gone far, so he backtracked, thinking he'd missed a turn. He found another path that led back the direction he'd come from, but it didn't lead to the room of doors, so he thought it must be the way.

After another dead end, another backtrack to a path that led to another dead end, Elend realized he was in a maze. But instead of finding his way in, he was already in the center and had to find his way out.

Doubt snuck up and poked at his shoulders, whispering that he was lost and not bright enough to remember the twists and turns of where he'd been. No wonder, really, why none of the tradesmen wanted him for an apprentice.

Elend hunched his shoulders against the whispers. "I can do this," he said, loudly, to drown them out.

His affirmation was weak and wobbly as a newborn calf, but he latched onto it, bolstering himself against the doubt.

With no difference he could see between the hedges or the stones from one path to another, he'd have to mark his way. He patted his pockets, but he had nothing in them. No bits of string or stub of chalk. No handy pebbles on the smooth pathway. He'd just have to mark the bushes then.

Elend broke off a largish branch from the nearest hedge.

The bush shrieked and shook its branches angrily, menacing. A long stem bent out and batted the broken piece out of Elend's hand. The hedge grew several inches, blocking his view of the apple trees.

He backed away from the offended hedge. "I'm so very sorry."

He hurried away in the general direction of the apple trees. Coming to yet another dead end, the tops of the trees just visible above, Elend had an idea.

"Maybe I'm not meant to solve it at all. Maybe I should break my way through."

He thought himself very clever. Until the bush in front of him puffed up, shook, then bristled with hundreds of needle-sharp thorns.

Right. No cheating.

"Well what am I to do then?" he cried, throwing up his hands.

The thorns retreated, the bush resuming its previous indifference to Elend's problem.

He supposed, eventually, the witch would realize her garden had been invaded, come to find him and, presumably, turn him into a toad or something. Or maybe he'd just wander the stupid maze until his stupid legs gave out and he'd die a stupid death all for the sake of a stupid apple and all so a stupid girl wouldn't think he was a stupid coward.

Stupid.

Elend had begun walking again while his thoughts wound round in his head. He scuffed his feet on the pavement, looking for stones to kick that weren't there and running his hand along the hedge. The leaves were glossy and smooth against his hand, shuffling when he —*skip*—brushed them . . .

Wait. *Skip*?

Elend hurried back to where he'd felt the interruption in the otherwise perfectly-trimmed hedge. He found an uneven spot where the hedges overlapped, cut to create the illusion of an unbroken line. Between them was a tunnel, just big enough for him to wiggle through.

He put his hand in first, flinching, waiting for the thorns to bristle out and impale him. When he remained unscathed, he shoved his arm through, then, going sideways, his body. And found himself on another path, parallel to the one he'd been on, a step closer to the apple trees.

With renewed hope and vigor, Elend put his hand back to the bushes and felt his way along until he found another overlap. Wiggling through that, he did it again, repeating the process, zig-zagging back and forth, going faster until he was running and laughing at his success.

Until he found not another opening, but a gate, and the apple trees just beyond.

"Good-bye maze! I have defeated you!" Was his battle cry as he rushed through the gate.

And the ground fell out from under his feet.

Elend's scream was cut short by the cold splash of water that enveloped his body. By the time he surfaced and finished coughing and panicking and yelling for help, he had no breath for anything but panting. His new problem was obviously a well, though it was larger —more the size of the fish pond in Hillcrest's only park —than any well he'd ever seen. But with its smooth, circular sides, and the rope and bucket far above his head, it could be nothing else.

Elend studied the sides, slick and smooth, like the marble columns of the rotunda in the town square. Then swam around, touching to confirm what his eyes told him; no hand or footholds in that unbroken, gray surface he could use to climb to the top. The well was wider than his outstretched arms, so he couldn't inch his way out; and taller than the miller's waterwheel, putting the bucket out of reach.

He swam down, feeling the sides under the water, searching for anything that might help, digging with fingers that only slid across the surface under his increasingly frantic scratching. He stayed under as long as he could, until his lungs burned, but that search was as fruitless as the first.

Elend returned to the center, coughing and gasping with more than the exertion of his swim. He tread water, arms and legs growing sluggish from his efforts, dread, and the chill seeping through his clothes and burrowing under his skin.

Fear, and with it despair, truly set in for the first time since he'd touched the garden gate latch. Elend's eyes stung and hot tears mingled with the frigid well water dripping from his hair down his cheeks. Here, in dark water who knew how deep, the sides too smooth to climb, and the top too far to jump for, he could only tread water for so long.

Through the looping thoughts of impending doom hopping in his head as thick as late summer grasshoppers in a grassy field, Elend heard the soft croon of Gran's voice. 'Relax', she told him. 'A panicked mind can't think clearly'.

He rolled onto his back to float as his gran had taught him when they swam together on hot summer days. Thinking of her calmed him; how she loved him and never thought of him as a failure, how patiently she taught him everything she knew. Elend would adopt Gran's patience and an answer would come to him. Hopefully.

With his ears underwater, the world took on a muffled silence, and his thoughts settled, drifting with the clouds that moved across the well opening. And they drifted in the direction of *why*. Why had he ended up at the bottom of a well?

Claren's goading for certain. But why? As the daisies had asked him, was it so very important what other people thought? Floating in what would be his death, with no help or hope in sight, it didn't seem very important at all.

But with the water closing off every other sound, leaving nothing but himself, Elend finally realized his problem.

Himself.

He let the opinions of others, of Claren, of Sarai, of the town, determine his own. He'd never once decided, for himself, who he was or who he wanted to be.

It seemed, to Elend, a rather unfortunate time for this epiphany, when it was too late to do anything about it. But that did seem to be the way of epiphanies.

No, it wasn't too late yet.

Elend righted himself in the water. He would search the sides of the well again. He would yell and yell for help until he couldn't yell anymore, or until the greenwitch found him. Maybe the garden would take pity and send a vine down for him to climb. He opened his mouth to do just that when a glow started and grew from the water below, illuminating his scissoring legs.

Out of the glow formed a face. One Elend had never seen before, but knew with the deep-down knowing that only blood and bone can know. The face was his father's. His father smiled, and in it, Elend saw himself.

"No!" Elend cried out, smacking at the water. "I will not be you. I *am* not you!"

He hit the water, punched it, again and again until the features were blurred with ripples and faded to nothing but light.

"I will be me." Elend panted.

Another face formed in the glow and Elend raised his fist again. He stopped, one arm above his head, when it became a woman's face with long hair floating around it. Another face he'd never seen before, but knew it for his mother's. She looked just like Gran.

Elend didn't like seeing her face either. She'd left him too, in her way. But he couldn't bring himself to punch her face into ripples and waves.

His mother's face looked down. When Elend looked too, he saw where the light was coming from; a tunnel, not far down. He swam to it, peeking inside. The light didn't stretch far back, but he thought he saw a shadow of stairs.

Elend came back up for air. He could make it to those stairs, but what if they didn't lead out? What if they weren't actually stairs? What if he couldn't hold his breath long enough to climb them?

He pressed his lips together, firmed his resolve. They *were* stairs, they *would* lead out, and he *could* hold his breath as long as needed to. For whatever reason, the garden had decided to help instead of hinder him. His imagination could have conjured up the images of his parents, but not that glow or his mother's face showing him the way out. Assistance was being offered and he wasn't too proud, or ungrateful, to accept.

After a whispered thanks to the magic he hoped was listening, he took several deep breaths then dove, kicking down as hard and fast as he could.

His mother's face smiled as he swam by and he thought she looked proud of him. Or maybe it was only that, for once, he felt proud of himself. Not only for who he was, but the person he now realized he could be.

He swam into the tunnel, using the bottom to push himself faster. The stairs were stairs, and they led up. He pushed off those too, flying upward, and broke into air before he realized he was close. His first gasp was startled rather than a need to breathe. But he sucked in another, then another, in belated gratitude to be above water and out of the well. He pulled himself out of the water and up the rest of the stairs to see where the garden had put him this time.

Inside a shed, it seemed.

He climbed out a hole in a dirt floor into the inside of a garden shed. Gardening tools, jars of seed, bags of fertilizer and potting soil, littered the floor in haphazard ways as if the owner had simply opened the door and thrown them in. And, thank all that was holy, and any god that might be listening, there was a door. One that opened easily when he turned the latch. He blinked against the bright sunlight.

Having learned his lesson, Elend took a good look outside that door before he moved forward. Studied the ground, even knelt to run his hands over and through the grass to make sure it was solid. He looked both right and left, and even remembered to look up. Seeing no threats, Elend drew deep breaths again and stepped out.

Outside was once again the wild garden. A grassy path led away from the shed, meandering to his left to tangle among vegetable plots. Behind him, the shed was gone, of course it was, in its place was another plot, this one of fruits. Round, fat, melons so ripe he could smell them. To his right was more vegetables and beyond them . . .

The apple trees.

He looked to the path, leading away, then back to the trees, and thought of everything that had happened since he stepped foot in the garden. He'd followed paths, whether he'd chosen to go or been forced down them, he'd followed.

Just like his whole life. Whether it was Claren's bullying, Sarai's lack of faith, or the tradesmen who wouldn't apprentice him, he'd accepted their judgment of him instead of showing them different.

Maybe he couldn't always choose his own path, but he could choose how he walked. And he decided, right then and there, to never be ashamed of being himself again.

The world shimmered around him, like the air on a hot and humid day. Shimmered and wavered, melted, and reformed. And he was standing under the shade of a tree. A sweet, cooling breeze blew over him, carrying the heavy smell of apples. A branch lowered to him, leaves luscious and green, nestling deep red fruits. Apples bigger than he'd ever seen. He could taste them, his teeth breaking the peel into the tart flesh, so full of juice it would run down his chin. He couldn't take his eyes off them. They were so beautiful, like a dream. He raised his hand to touch the apple, skin warm from the sun. To grasp it and pull—

"What have we here?"

Elend stumbled away from the tree, the voice jolting him out of the trance. Something snagged at his foot and he fell, his tailbone hitting hard.

"Always remember, it's the roots that will trip you while you're staring at the treetops," said the woman who seemed to have appeared out of nowhere.

She was dressed simply, in a blouse and a skirt tied up nearly to her knees. Her bare feet were muddy, dirt smudged her shirt, more streaked her forehead. Her hair, which wasn't gray but pale blonde, was piled atop her head in a lopsided bun in danger of coming apart.

The greenwitch.

She wasn't that old at all, Elend thought, not as old as his gran anyway. And if it weren't for her eyes, she might have been the ma of any child in the village. But her eyes, cold, like bluebells caught in an early frost, were on him and glittering with a strange light.

"What are you then?" she asked softly, dangerously. "Visitor or thief?"

Elend scrambled to his feet and began to back away. "I—well, that is—I didn't mean—"

The witch stretched out a hand, and Elend froze, waiting for the lightning strike. His face scrunched, but eyes slit open. She only brushed a leaf on a low hanging branch.

"Tell me the truth, child. I'll know if you lie."

While the witch waited, eyebrows raised, Elend opened his mouth, then closed it when nothing came out. Then he tried again. When he tried a third time with no success, she heaved a sigh, plucked a leaf, and, quicker than he thought anyone should be able to move, shoved the leaf into his mouth.

"Loosen his tongue," she commanded.

All the words trapped inside came pouring out. He told her about Claren's insults, the dare, and all his trials from the gate opening to approaching the trees. All of it, in more detail than he remembered.

"But I wasn't going to steal any, I swear," he finished. "Or at least I didn't want to . . ." He shot a nervous glance at the tree. "It enchanted me!"

"Of course it did," she snapped in a tone that questioned his intelligence. "It's my tree in my garden and I'm a greenwitch. Blood sacrifices, eh?"

Elend nodded vigorously, as if the force of his agreement could convince her of his truthfulness.

"I wouldn't touch that dark magic, so calm yourself." Her eyes swept the garden thoughtfully, then came back to him. "And the gate opened for you, did it?"

"Yes, ma'am." More enthusiastic nodding.

"I see. What is your name?"

"Elend, ma'am. Elend Treefell."

"Well, Elend Treefell, my name is Marteen Larkspur, and you have had quite an adventure." She stepped aside and gestured to the tree. "You may take an apple."

He'd expected to be struck down, maybe returned to the well, or transformed into a toad. Or marched straight to his gran, which would have been worse than anything the witch could do.

"Ma'am?"

"You braved the greenwitch's lair, Elend Treefell, and fought your way through the garden. Doesn't every successful quest win a reward? Go on. Take one."

Elend slowly walked to the tree, keeping a wary eye on the witch in case of a trick. But she only nodded and the tree lowered a branch laden with red fruit. Elend picked out an especially large, glossy one, already envisioning shoving it in Claren's smirking face.

But then he thought of the garden gate locking behind him. And how this very tree had entranced him only minutes before. Even though the witch offered it freely, he had a sudden, certain feeling something bad would happen if he picked that apple.

And if he took it, if he gave it to Claren, wouldn't that mean he still thought he had to prove himself? Elend was done following that path.

"No ma'am," he said, dropping his hand and stepping away. This time watching the ground for roots. "I thank you for the offer, but . . . no."

"You're not stealing, I'm giving it to you."

"I understand. But I don't want it anymore. And I'm sorry for intruding in your garden."

Her blue eyes thawed but were just as unsettling when she studied him closely. As if she could read his heart.

"Well. If you won't have an apple, how about some cookies? I have lavender and lemon. And I'll clean your cuts while you eat. That's a nasty one on your wrist."

Examining himself, Elend found that while the well had left him wet, it hadn't done much to clean him.

Marteen walked away without waiting for his agreement and he hurried to catch up. She made her way on a straight gravel path that cut the garden in half and led to her cottage.

"Tricky garden," he muttered, then jumped over a cucumber vine that tried to catch his ankle. "Ma'am?"

"Yes, Elend?"

A bush with purple cone flowers swung a branch to smack his arm. Its leaf, broad with jagged edges, snagged and caught on his shirt.

"Hey!"

The greenwitch snapped her fingers. "That's enough now. You've had your fun, and he's a guest." She glanced over her shoulder, ignoring the shiver of leaves that sounded suspiciously like a rustling giggle. "You had a question?"

"Yes, um—" He kept an eye on the bushes until they were well behind him. "What would have happened if I'd taken an apple?"

"I would have had one less apple."

"Well, yes, but I guess I mean . . . what if I'd eaten it?"

"That's a different question entirely. And a much smarter one." She turned her head, not quite looking at him, though he felt her attention all the same. "Why do you ask?"

"It didn't seem right. I had a feeling, you see, a bad one and—that sounds stupid."

This time she did turn and grab his shoulders. He shrank away from the power once again in her eyes.

"It is not stupid at all, Elend. I believe very much in strong feelings. You did well to follow yours."

Instead of taking the lead again, she put her arm through his so they walked together, as if he were a grown-up. Someone important. Elend stood up straight and tall.

"When I pick the apples and bake with them, they are ordinary fruits in ordinary food, except for the spells I work into the baking. But, plucked and eaten straight from the tree, they are powerful. Many things might have happened. You might have seen your future, your greatest achievement, or your greatest tragedy. You might have been granted a wish."

"That doesn't sound so bad."

"Doesn't it? Wishes are rarely granted in the way we would like because so often we don't know what our hearts truly desire. And the future is something best kept to itself. We should make our own choices, Elend, don't you think?" He glanced up at her. He didn't remember telling her of his epiphany. "If you had known all of what would befall you in this garden, you might not have come. And we wouldn't be having this nice conversation."

He thought about that for a few steps, then asked, "Would you have let me take an apple?"

"Once the choice was yours, free of compulsion, yes."

Elend shivered, thinking of what might have happened. Obviously, the greenwitch believed if people intentionally played with magic, they deserved what they got.

Soon they arrived at the cottage, and Marteen directed him to a bucket of water with a basket beside it. "Wash up here, especially around those cuts on your hands. I'll get us some tea."

"Yes, ma'am."

Elend took special care in washing and brushing as much dirt off his clothes as possible, even though Marteen hadn't joined him to clean up herself. She probably spelled the mud not to fall off until she told it to. His gran would love a spell like that.

When he turned from the bucket, she was arranging two trays on a small table; one with bandages and pots, the other with a tea service and cookies.

He hadn't noticed the table and chairs on his first trip through, though he had been distracted and could have missed them. What he did know was that the witch hadn't had time to gather the trays while he washed. And he would have sworn she hadn't entered the cottage.

"Well, come and sit before the tea gets cold," Marteen said.

Elends stomach grumbled, telling him it was silly to worry about magic tea services after talking flowers and wells that glowed with the faces of his parents. And that it was hungry.

Marteen poured out the tea, whispering words too soft for Elend to understand, and placed four cookies,

two yellow and two purple, on a plate before taking his
hand to tend to the cuts. Elend chose a yellow cookie
and lemon filled his mouth and nose, mingling with the
lavender aroma of the tea and the more stringent odor
of the ointment.

The witch hummed while she worked, and Elend
ate, the tea and cookies easing his stomach and
calming his emotions together. Soothed, and tired from
the day's events, Elend found himself drowsy. When
she finished with one hand and reached for the other,
he realized it lay on the table, limply holding a half-
eaten cookie. She filled his cup to warm the tea that
had grown cool before ministering his other hand.

"Elend, why didn't you take the apple?" she asked
softly amid her humming.

"My father," he said, then jerked up straight, wide
awake once more. "Did you spell me?"

"No, just waited for a time you'd tell me the truth.
The whole truth," she amended when he sputtered a
protest. "What about your father?"

"I wanted that apple because of what Claren said,
because I was ashamed. But I don't need it. I'm not my
father and I don't have to prove that to anyone."

Marteen smoothed ointment on a larger cut, then
blew on it to take away the sting when Elend flinched.
"He wasn't all bad. Not a responsible bone in his body,
mind you, or one to think of anyone but himself, but
not evil."

"You knew him? But you've only lived here a few
years."

"That's a story for another time," she said, patting
his hand before letting him have it so he could eat with
both. "You'll have a bit of him, your mother as well,

and even more of your gran since she's had the raising of you. And all of it together will give you the pieces of who Elend will be. That's what you'll decide, and that's what's important."

With her work done, she poured out tea for herself and took a cookie before putting the rest on his plate.

"So, Elend, who will you be? You're old enough now to be apprenticed, I imagine?"

"Well, yes." He put the cookie he'd just been ready to bite back on the plate. He'd promised himself to never be ashamed again and was now receiving his first lesson in how the making of promises was so much easier than the keeping. "Almost no one will have me, see? And the ones who've offered, Gran won't allow."

A spark of anger lit her blue eyes, but only a moment before her expression turned crafty. "Does your gran like me, Elend?"

His stomach jumped from discomfort to discomfort, shame to nerves to fear. The greenwitch had been kind, sure—well at least after he'd convinced her he wasn't a thief—but what if this was the real trick? What if he made her angry? What if—

Her laugh interrupted his churning attempts to figure out what to say. "Tell me the truth, boy, like before, it's all I want." She tapped his hand with a finger. "Long ago, I came to the same realization as you; I am more than what my blood would make me. I'm comfortable in my skin, you won't hurt my feelings."

"Well, I-I don't know that she actually *likes* you. But she does say you're powerful and to be respected. And that it's good for Hillcrest to have its own greenwitch."

The witch's eyes went far away, like Gran's
sometimes did when she talked of his grandfather, long
dead. Or his ma. Her smile was wistful. "That's fair
praise from Amala Treefell," she said, then her
attention sharpened once more. "And what do you
think she would say to you being apprenticed to me?"

"But I'm not a witch!"

"Not such as you're thinking, but—"

She grabbed his wrist, his cuts throbbing, then
burning with the heat in her fingers. A static built at
the back of his neck, like before the crack of lightning,
and sparkled down his arm to snap at her hand.

She rocked back in her chair but didn't break her
hold. A sudden wind blew at her, ripping more strands
from her already precarious bun. The garden gate
rattled in distress, and the greenwitch laughed.

"All right then, settle down. Nothing to get all riled
up about." She released Elend and took up her teacup,
smiling the smug smile of the vindicated. "I thought
there might be some power in your bloodline. My
garden doesn't open for just anyone."

"What was that?" Elend asked, a little afraid and a
little excited. "What do you mean?"

"A small display," she said, waving a dismissive
hand. "Nothing to worry about. As for what it means?
That there is a great deal I can teach you. So, what say
you? Shall I talk to your gran?"

Elend nodded. Not because of the magic he might
have—he couldn't, quite, believe in that yet—but
because of the garden that had let him in. The garden
that had tested him, comforted him, and hurt him—a
little—as it taught him. And because of the greenwitch,

too. A person who walked her own path seemed a fine
teacher to help him find his.

"Yes, ma'am."

"Then you may now call me Mistress." She clapped
her hands then rubbed them together as she rose to her
feet. "Next order of business. What shall it be? Frog?
Snake? Maybe a fish? Young boys like slimy, squirmy
things don't they?"

Elend froze halfway to standing himself. What
could she mean? A familiar? Did apprentices have one?
That seemed more a graduation gift sort of thing.
"Mistress?"

"What would you like to be?" She explained
patiently. "I can't imagine a frog would be much fun,
just sitting around and croaking, though I could see the
appeal of a fish. Perhaps a salamander? There's a
lovely rock arrangement in the back garden you could
explore."

"But I thought I was to be your apprentice," he
blurted out.

"A simple transformation for the rest of the day, not
forever," Marteen reassured him, though her frown,
caused by his assumption, made him wary. "I can't
have any other daring children believe they can brave
the greenwitch's garden without consequences. So
what form would you like to explore? There's nothing
quite like a good transformation to get you looking at
the world in a new way."

Searching for inspiration, Elend looked around then
up and saw two birds swooping and swirling around
one another. "A bird. I want to fly."

"Excellent choice." Marteen tapped a finger to her
lips. "What kind?"

"A hawk?" Elend suggested, picturing himself as the fierce, brave bird.

Marteen raised a questioning eyebrow. "Are you squeamish about eating mice and snakes? You'll need a snack, flying is hard work."

The tea and cookies soured in his stomach. "No thank you, Mistress."

"How about a cardinal? The snacks are palatable, if bland, and I'll be able to keep track of you by your color."

Not very exciting, Elend thought, but better than a sparrow. And he could hardly be disappointed by her choice when it was her spell that meant he'd be able to fly. He nodded his agreement.

"Let's get on with it then, if I'm to have time to visit your gran and explain why you'll be missing supper."

Elend ducked his head, shame and fear overcoming his newfound excitement. "Do you have to tell her everything?"

"How else will I explain our meeting and my wish to make you my apprentice? Don't worry, child, I shall be the most contented victim of thievery there ever was, and indeed, grateful for your intrusion." Marteen winked at him. "Now. Put on a good show, Elend."

Before he could ask what she meant, she opened her mouth and screeched. She flicked a finger to fling a tray into the garden gate, blasting it open, scattering bandages and ointment pots.

"That's your cue," Marteen said.

Elend realized she wanted theatrics, and he scurried for the gate. With Marteen following, furiously throwing threats and dire warnings at him, he only needed to half pretend to flee from her wrath for the other children still waiting by the miller's door. To Elend, the trip through the garden had seemed to last a lifetime, but hardly any time must have passed at all. Once he was on the road, Elend felt a crackling that raised every hair on his body.

"Let this be a lesson!" the greenwitch yelled.

Her spell hit him square between the shoulder blades, knocking him to the dirt. It took several, floundering seconds to realize it wasn't arms flailing for balance or toes scrabbling for purchase, but claws scratching and feathers fluttering.

Without him telling his new body what to do, even if he knew what to tell it, he hopped to his feet. Wings tucked to his side, he cocked his head to see the children scatter, running for the hill.

All except for Sarai, who stood with her mouth open, hands fisted at her sides. Until Minea grabbed her sister's arm to pull her away.

"Well done, Elend," the greenwitch said. He couldn't tilt his head back to see much more than her muddy leg beside him. She crouched down and pulled an apple from the folds of her skirt. "It's charmed and harmless. My gift and your proof."

His feathers fluffed and he opened his beak to chirp a sharp trill at her.

"I know you don't need it for yourself. But it will keep that nasty boy's mouth shut for a time at least, eh?" He answered her laugh with staccato whistles. "Off with you then."

She lifted him so he could dig his claws into the fruit, then opened her hands. He spread his wings and flapped for all he was worth, expecting to need more strength than his small wings had to carry the apple.

But it was light—lighter than a seed, than a blade of grass, than bright new hopes.

His frantic flapping sent him skidding across the dirt as he tried to figure out the mechanics of flying. Then the magic shoved his mind to the side and he was up, winging his way after the fleeing children.

Sarai called his name as he flew by, low enough to ruffle Minea's hair and make her laugh. He circled them once before diving after Claren. The boy looked over his shoulder, legs pumping faster when he saw the cardinal coming for him. Elend swept past him then turned in a wide arc, wanting to see Claren's face.

Before they could collide, Elend back winged and dropped the apple right in Claren's path. The boy screamed and jerked so hard to avoid fruit and spelled-bird both that his feet skidded out from under him, dropping him on his backside in the road.

Singing out his laughter, Elend flew back the way he had come, swooping and spinning in the air, intoxicated by the wind in his wings.

He circled the greenwitch then skimmed over her garden before aiming for the clouds. Higher and higher he climbed until the treetops, the town draped over a hill, and a running group of children were small. Tiny dots in his new, wide world.

————

K.D. Kelley resides with her husband and two boys in the wilds of the Kansas Flint Hills. She finds inspiration in abandoned prairie homesteads, the shadows between hay bales and hedgerows, and other quiet, lost places. The results have appeared in various short story magazines and anthologies.

MÉRE'S WORDS

EDDIE CANTRELL

Each night when Belle lay on her moth-eaten mattress in the servants' quarters and pulled the paper-thin sheet up to her chin, she drifted back to her mother, her beloved *mére*. In the cool and dank darkness, Belle dreamed of sun-kissed afternoons on the puffy-as-a-summer-cloud couch, with a book spread open on Mére's lap, Belle's head on her mother's shoulder.

Mére's words always began with '*Once upon a time, far, far away . . .*'. Chewing on bites of Turkish delight and watching her mother's lips move, Belle's mouth used to turn up into a smile and her eyes twinkled with warmth, knowledge and mischief. On those glowing words, Belle drifted off the couch, out the window and up, up over Paris to wherever Mére's words took her.

Belle had been away so long that her mother's face had started to fade from memory but Mére's words, oh, she could never forget those words, and so she could never forget her *mére*.

Tonight, Belle lay shivering in the servants' quarters under the château. Not because of the chill though — her *mére's* words kept her warm from the inside. For the first time since being brought to *le Château de la*

Lune on that rainy winter's day, Belle wasn't cold. Or afraid. She was elated.

A month ago, Belle had woken up in the middle of the night to find Mére sitting next to her. Although the quarters were shrouded in darkness, Mére was bright as sunshine. Belle had sat wide-eyed, heart pounding.

"*Ma mére,*" she whispered with a huge smile.

For a long moment Mére did nothing but warm her only child, her best friend, her *petite lapine* with a smile that promised a tale and bite of Turkish delight. She leaned forward and whispered in Belle's ear. Belle felt her mother's warm breath on her skin.

"Come back, Belle. I don't have much longer left, *ma petite lapine*, my little rabbit. But your friend in the woods can help me . . . like you helped her. The very next time the night sky dances with the full moon, come back to Paris. Prepare, Belle. I'm waiting for you. The two of you." Then Mére had stood up and walked out the door, footsteps retreating in the passage before silence returned.

Belle took a deep breath hoping to quiet her racing heart for just a moment longer. *Tonight, my Mére, tonight!* She knew well what happened to servants who dared to leave the *château.* This place was evil. But Mére needed her.

All the other breathing in the cramped quarters had settled into the slow rhythm of slumber, but still Belle waited. Words twirled from her mind in a serpentine kaleidoscope, weaving a new tale, only this one was of her own making.

Deep in the forest stands the ancient tree. Within its hollow belly lies a stolen jewellery box. In the stolen jewellery box rests my best friend—my best friend with the broken wing. Belle's smile widened. "I'm coming, Clara. You and I are escaping this horrible *château* tonight. I promise you."

For a moment, Belle felt emptiness, the same emptiness she had felt ever since those quiet days when the illness yellowed Mére's skin and she could no longer read the book of fairy tales. Eventually the tall men in the black automobile with the black chugging smoke came to take Belle from Paris. Mére's last words were not spoken but written. She had placed them in Belle's hand as the men pulled them apart.

But now, Belle had hope.

"Clara," Belle had asked her new friend in the woods, "will you heal my *mére* like you healed my scraped knees and my aching tummy? Will you help my *mére* like I helped you when I found you with your wing broken?"

"Of course, I will."

Belle looked at the three sleeping shapes around her, each on their own mattress, huddled in the moonlit gloom.

She shifted to the edge of her own mangy mattress and sat up. Her hands found and slid the cloth sling bag out from between the wall and the head of the mattress. From it, she pulled out the three lilies she had picked in the forest that afternoon. Two of the white lilies were gently tied together at the stems with twine. Belle leaned over to the mattress next to hers and placed the flowers on the pillow. A wisp of warm breath caressed her fingers as she pulled her hand away. *Au revoir, Aimée. I will miss you, mon amie.*

As Belle stood, one of the older girls across from her, Geneviéve, coughed in her sleep. Belle froze, eyes wide. Geneviéve and her mean-as-skunk-stink friend Stéphanie would be serious problems if they woke. Whenever Stéphanie sniggered, spoke or glared, she did so with generous measures of venom, and she reserved a special portion of her venom for *le rat de la ville—the city rat.*

The last thing Belle needed was to wake Stéphanie. Oh, it would please that nasty piece of work so to catch her sneaking out of the servants' quarters again. The last time that happened, Stéphanie went straight to Madame Desjardin who proceeded to make Belle kneel on a scatter of roughly-ground salt for six hours. The time before that, she received a serious whipping.

But to Stéphanie's dismay, the nasty slashes healed completely within two days. Even Belle was surprised. Ever since that morning when Belle had been sent hunting for wild mushrooms and found Clara lying in the dead leaves at the foot of the ancient tree, her life had changed in mysterious ways. The more time she spent with Clara, nursing her broken wing, the more Belle's coughs disappeared, cuts vanished, and aches went as quickly as they came.

But not everyone's wounds healed.

Belle gazed at the empty mattress to her left. No sheets, no pillow but the soft impressions could still be seen in the moonlight. Isabelle had been a quiet girl, slight of build. Although she'd rarely spoken, her eyes would light up whenever Belle talked about her favourite fairy-tales. Issy had been a believer, too.

But then she'd tried to escape.

"Oh, Issy." The beatings at the *château* were reaching new levels of brutality and the countess,

Madame Desjardin, enforced her rules with an iron
fist. Belle placed the third lily on Isabelle's mattress.

She stood up, bag slung over her back, and tip-toed
out of the corner, across the wooden floors beneath the
fat, milky moon framed by the large window, and past
the others, curled up in their sheets.

The door glided open without a creak. The blob of
grease Belle stole from the work shed this afternoon
did its job well.

She took one step out of the room and paused in the
doorway. *Don't! Don't you dare look back, Belle. Not
now. You have to forget about Aimée for now and
think about Clara. About Mére.* Belle grit her teeth and
took another step but—

"Where do you think you are going . . . *rat de la
ville?*"

Belle spun around.

Stéphanie's silhouette sat upright on her mattress
like a black tombstone on a grave.

"I'm . . . I'm," Belle stuttered.

"Going on one of your little adventures into the
woods again, mmm? Ten years old and still believes in
magic." Stéphanie sniggered.

"No, I . . . I need the lavatory. That's all."

Geneviéve, too, uncoiled from her sheet to a sitting
position. *Great*, Belle thought.

"Ooooo, little city rat is going to find—what did she
call it? Ah! The light that floats in the woods. Her
fairy." Geneviéve said. Both girls giggled and flapped
their hands in mocking flight.

"She found a bird," came a voice across from
Stéphanie.

Aimée! Unlike the other girls, sleep did not sprinkle her voice. *Was she awake the whole time? Does she know I'm leaving?*

"A swallow chick fell out of her nest and Belle is nursing her. What's wrong with that, Stéphanie?" Aimée never let her anger show. Her calm was a weapon.

"She's running after childish fantasies. Like always. And whenever she gets caught, it's us that get punished," Stéphanie said, her voice a hissing whisper.

"No, I'm just going to the lavatory. I promise."

"Liar!" Geneviéve said, her voice rising. "And I'm going to tell. Right now!" She flung the sheet from her legs but when Aimée spoke in her calm voice, the girl paused.

"Then I'll tell Madame Desjardin where I found the four stolen pieces of chocolate cake. The pieces that were meant for Madame Desjardin's sons." Aimée sat up and yawned loudly. "How did the chocolate cake taste, girls? I have never even tasted chocolate cake. Have you, Belle?"

"No," Belle said, but who needed chocolate cake when you could have Turkish delight?

Stéphanie and Geneviéve's postures stiffened but were followed by thick silence.

"Go then. See if we care. You'll get caught, city rat," Stéphanie snapped and lay back down. "And when you get dragged back to the *château*, I'll be waiting to welcome you back. Good night."

Geneviéve flung the sheet over herself to Stéphanie's hissed cackles.

Anger rose and Belle took a step toward the girls. She had never in the years since coming ever spoken back to them. Until now. "Not if *Les Hidieux* have their way with you two first."

The girls burst into hushed laughter. Not the reaction Belle was hoping for and for a moment, humiliation warmed her face. No one believed in them, but Belle did. Mére always said there were more than just fairies and pixies. Vampires and werewolves roamed this world, too. So did witches and monsters. *"Where goodness flourishes, evil lurks not far behind."*

"Actually, rat," Stéphanie sang in a deep baritone and rose up on her mattress, sheet draped over her body. "*Les Hidieux*, the demeeeeented shaaaaadows in the waaaaalls and cellars of *Le Château de la Looooon* are comiiiiinnnngg to murder any servant girl trying to escape. Just assssk pooooor Isabelle."

Geneviéve laughed as Stéphanie fell onto her mattress and wrapped her sheet around her throat and proceeded to make choking sounds.

Hopefully the darkness hid the red blush glowing from her face. "Good bye," Belle whispered but did not look at Aimée before stepping into the darkness of the passage. *I'll come back for you. I promise.*

The door swung shut behind her. Mére always said the best stories were the simplest ones. What Belle needed to do was keep the story simple.

Walk down the passage, climb the staircase to the ground floor and sneak into the kitchen. Steal the cherries and cheese, then creep out the back door into the garden. Run across the garden and disappear into the forest. After that, it's simply get Clara from the ancient tree and then reach the train station. Belle had planned everything. The plan *had* to work.

Belle took a breath, smiled and turned to the passage. Her smile faded. During the day, this passage was a measly ten steps long. In the gloom however, it stretched into forever.

Belle clutched her bag to her chest and skittered on her tip-toes down the passage. Halfway there, a rush of cold air wrapped around her ankles. She stumbled to a stop with a gasp and glanced at the heavily-bolted door to her right. Rumour had it that the door led to the dark and never-ending cellars under the *château*. A hiss sputtered from under the crack, followed by a long, sinister scraping down the length of the door.

Fear numbed her legs into dough.

Behind the door, the rabid creatures frantically sniffed and scratched. The smell of her fear excited them.

In a panic, life surged through her legs. She whipped around and ran through the dark passage. Behind her, louder and louder thuds pounded the cellar door.

Belle skidded around the corner. Ahead of her was an ascending staircase.

"Who is running around down there?"

Belle jumped back around the corner, breath trapped in her chest.

"I asked, who is down there?" The voice was shrill as that of an angry stray cat in the night. Madame Desjardin.

Belle looked back down the passage. *If she catches me, she'll whip my hands raw and dunk them in vinegar.*

Something sharp—a high-heel maybe—stabbed on the first step. "Is it one of you servant girls?" Another step. "You know what happens to servants caught snooping around the *château* at night."

Belle pressed herself against the wall. The Countess Desjardin came alive at night. She always prowled around the *château* like a sadistic prison warden.

The staircase remained quiet. After a few agonising moments, Madame Desjardin huffed and Belle heard her sharp footsteps snap along the wooden floorboards in the entrance hall before finally disappearing somewhere into the building.

Belle peeped around the corner and released a long breath. She flicked her wispy fringe back and slowly took the staircase up to the entrance hall.

Moonlight gushed through the long windows and black shadows stained the wide-open entrance hall.

Belle took the last steps out onto the hall's varnished wood floor. The double entrance doors beckoned, but she needed food for the train trip to Paris and Clara was still weak. The wild cherries in the pantry would heal her.

After one last look around the room, Belle tip-toed through the gloom to the kitchen. The door stood slightly ajar. She crept through the doorway after making sure the coast was clear.

A long, bulky wooden table with six sturdy chairs stood in the middle of the room. The swirling smells of the kitchen greeted her. Strings of braided garlic, onions and peppers hung from the ceiling as well as logs of cured meat and sausage. Bushes of basil and rosemary sat in their pots on the window sill. So did a big bowl of wild cherries Belle had to pick earlier that afternoon She was reprimanded, though, for picking some which were still not ripe enough, and so the bowl was placed on the windowsill for the fruit to ripen.

Belle quickly crept passed the cast-iron pots hanging above the fire stove toward the pantry cupboard. She lay the fabric bag open across the table, grabbed two handfuls of cherries and emptied them into the bag. Then she turned around and opened the pantry.

Moonlight revealed all the glass jars and tins. Ignoring the many shelves with their perishable delights, she went straight for the big jars of nuts and dried fruit. A sweet, floral smell with a tinge of spiciness that she couldn't quite place tingled her nostrils, but there was no time to ponder its source.

She grabbed handfuls of dried apricots and apple, darted out of the cupboard and dumped the fruit in the bag before darting back in for the two small hunks of cheese. Then Belle snatched two long logs of sausage off their hooks. Sausage was only for elite visitors or Madame Desjardin's spoiled children . . . or her 'late-night' visitors. Now, they would be for a servant girl and her mother. *If you get caught, Belle, you'll be whipped to death—*

Something shiny on the top shelf of the pantry cupboard caught her eye. A smile spread. There they were. Nicely wrapped in pink boutique paper–the source of the sweet, flowery smell. Turkish delights, all the way from Bordeaux! Madame Desjardin's personal favourite.

Belle's too. And Mére's.

No, Belle. You have enough food. It's time to go. Now.

But Belle licked her lips. She reached down, slid the wooden step out from under the last shelf and placed it in the right spot. She stood on the tips of her toes and grabbed a handful of the sweets. Paper crinkled as her fingers curled around the soft, gelatine sweets. The taste practically travelled through the wrapping into her pores and exploded on her taste buds. Belle jumped off the step, clutching her prize.

Just one for now. Just one, I promise. The rest are for Mère. Maybe Clara will also like them—

A tall, spindly silhouette loomed in the pantry's doorway, black as a widow spider.

"I knew it was you, Belle," Madame Desjardin said. Her voice grated like a coffin being dragged across the floor.

Limb-numbing fear gripped Belle and she bit her lower lip. *Belle, you silly girl! How could you be so lost in the clouds? You should've been keeping an ear out!*

Madame Desjardin raised her long, deathly-thin hands. "Get over here!" Tentacle-like fingers snapped toward Belle. "Oh, I know the right place for you," she said as her face twisted with detestation and anger. "Let's see if those childish fairy tales will do you any good in the cellar."

Belle ducked under the snapping hands. She scrambled forward, slipping and sliding in a panic and accidentally slammed her shoulder into Madame Desjardin's side which sent the woman clattering into the kitchen table.

The woman's eyes flashed. "You . . . you evil, little city tramp!"

"No, I didn't mean to!" Belle screamed and dove for the bag of food on the table. Madame Desjardin did too, but Belle got there first and pulled the items out of the woman's reach.

"How dare you, ungrateful *merde*! That is mine!"

Belle turned for the back door. Sharp nails snatched at her back, ripping her clothing and pulling out clumps of her hair as she tore away. She knocked over several of the wooden chairs behind her as she fled and Madame Desjardin bowled into the furniture, toppling over. "Aargh! You have made a grave mistake, you cancerous brat!"

Belle flung open the back door and ran out into a cool, starlit night.

A long stretch of manicured lawn spread out ahead of her toward the tall wrought-iron fence at the edge of the garden. It was a straight, easy dash to the woods, and then freedom.

Behind her, furniture clattered and clanged and Madame Desjardin emerged from the *château*. "Guards!" she shrieked. "Guards! A runaway! You'll never outrun them, you brat!"

Belle broke into a sprint. *You'll never outrun them.* Belle knew well who she meant. The soft lawn wet from the day's rain squished under her bare feet.

"*Run, ma petite lapine. Run like that imagination of yours.*"

The wind roared in her ears and rushed over her face. *I'm coming ma mére. I'm coming, Clara.*

Two dark shapes tore around the wall of the *château* to her left. Her smile faltered.

Guttural growls swelled as the two dark shapes grew closer, grew larger.

The dogs. The savage guardians of the *château* with their glistening black pelts, small eyes bursting with bloodlust, and studded collars clinging around thick muscular necks. They pursued her, jowls curled back around endless rows of jagged, sharp teeth, ribbons of saliva trailing from their wide, hideous jaws. Angry barks filled the night.

Every servant girl remembered what these beasts did to young Rebecca two years ago. No servant girl could forget. Madame Desjardin made sure that every girl in the *château* saw what happened to servants who tried escaping.

Her legs that a moment ago seemed to drive her on faster than a hare, now betrayed her with their weakness.

The two hounds fell in on her flank.

"Damian! Fedor! Get her, *mes bonbons*! Get her!" Madame Desjardin screamed.

Belle let out a low cry as their jaws snapped at her heels.

Mére's voice rose up and urged her. *"Ma petite lapine! Remember how brave Irene was in the face of the goblins! Do not be a damsel in distress. Be a warrior princess!"*

Belle glanced over her shoulder. The dogs tripped and stumbled over each other, fighting to get a bite out of her. She grabbed the two logs of cured meat from the bag and flung them at the dogs.

First, one stopped and sniffed the meat. Then the other skidded to a halt. Like all of Madame Desjardin's servants, they were kept hungry too and started fighting over the meat.

Relief pushed Belle forward. The fence was only a few feet away. *Nearly there!*

A sharp, high-pitched whistle sliced the night. Belle risked another glance over her shoulder. *What was that?*

Madame Desjardin lowered something small from her lips. A whistle.

The two dogs looked toward the house, ears pricked up.

A deep trembling rose up from the earth and shook her bones. A sudden hiss of wind rushed from the house, across the lawn. It whooshed up over Belle's body and blew her hair across her face.

"*Les Hidieux*," she said in a shaky voice.

Terror slammed into Belle and she gave a tiny moan. No one had ever seen them but she knew they existed, even when the other girls mocked her for it.

She whispered the only word that could give her the courage to move, the single word that brought a flicker of light even in the most impenetrable darkness.

"Mére."

All the shutters of *le Château de la Lune* rattled and slammed against the building and the trembling became a rumble. Belle ran as panicked screams reached out of the *château's* rooms. The rumbles became the clear sounds of scuttering footsteps and frantic breathing. Somewhere behind her, the dogs darted off, yelping like puppies.

The footsteps grew louder. Belle ran to the fence. *Don't look back. Just get over this fence!*

A swelling, deep-throated growl filled her ears followed by a blood-curling whisper. "*Belle. Ma petite lapine,*" *Les Hidieux* mocked in hungry tones.

Belle flung the bag over the fence, sprang forward, and wedged her foot onto a cross-beam. As she heaved herself up, something cold closed around her ankles and pulled down.

Belle screeched and kicked back. Her heel struck something tough and leathery. The entity hissed angrily and let go.

Belle grit her teeth, grabbed another cross-beam and slipped over the top of the two-meter high fence, its sharp points scraping her belly. She crashed to the ground on the other side and scrambled away on hands and knees in case anything tried to grab and pull her back.

Breathing heavily and heart pounding, Belle grabbed the bag and sprinted to the awaiting darkness of the woods. Safe in the gloom and chill of the forest, she darted behind a pine tree and dared to look back at the monsters.

Only there was nothing there.

Belle blinked. Frowned. *But, but . . . I felt the earth trembling and, and . . .*

No savage, reptilian creatures. No shadowy beings with glowing red eyes. Belle shot glances around the grounds. The two dogs still fed on the sausages on the lawn.

But they ran off, I saw them run off.

Light flickered in the *château's* windows now and Madame Desjardin could be heard screaming from somewhere inside for the groundsmen to bring more hunting dogs.

The urge to run gnawed at her, but Belle hesitated, hands glued to the tree, feet stuck to the cool forest earth. *Where are they? They were right there! I know they were. I felt them. I heard them.*

Stéphanie cackled in her ear. *"Fairy tales, rat de la ville. Silly, pathetic words to make you feel better. But you are nothing more than a dirty servant girl whose mother abandoned her. Now you fill your days with your head in the clouds."*

Belle shut her eyes and shook her head.

Shouting and barking rang from the *château*. Belle looked up. A small gang of men and hunting dogs tore around the corner of the building. The long, praying-mantis shape of Madame Desjardin glided across the lawn toward the men and pointed in Belle's direction.

Belle swung the bag around her and ran deeper into the forest. Her magic friend was waiting for her. There was no way Belle would abandon her, just like there was no way her *mére* could ever abandon Belle. Never.

Dogs barking and men shouting in the not-so-far distance trickled through the trees and bushes. Belle zig-zagged around fat oaks and slender pines. She ducked under fallen trees and hopped over large rocks. Night birds squawked and animals scuttled in the bushes.

Deeper into the forest she went. In the white beams of moonlight, the secret parts of the forest came to life. Here, her imagination was at its most vivid. This was another world where pixies sat on giant red mushrooms, glittering fairies drifted through the trees, and even unicorns and dragons roamed. The sounds of her pursuers became a distant, almost insignificant murmur. Surely, they would never find her here.

Belle reached a thick tangle of shrubs and thorn bushes formed a wall of foliage. This barrier stopped those without the magic to see the way through, but Belle had found it. She dropped to her hands and knees and crawled under the foliage through a semi-circular tunnel.

When she emerged on the other side, she stood up to a thickly-trunked tree that twisted and twirled up into a broad tangle of branches as gnarled as the fingers of an old and wise wizard. At the base of the trunk, a labyrinth of fat roots parted to form a wide, open mouth. The ancient tree.

Warmth and joy and excitement tingled through Belle's body. For so long, she had tried to find the words to describe the ancient tree. *I can't wait to tell Mére about you.*

Belle crouched among the roots that led into the ancient tree's belly and reached for the items she had hidden here ages ago—the candle and small box of matches. She lit the candle. A soft radiance flickered across the wooden skin of the tree.

"Clara, I'm coming." Belle held the candle to the opening and took a step into the belly of the tree.

"She's here somewhere!" a voice boomed, followed by a barrage of barking.

Belle swung around. *No! How did they get here? That's impossible! Only those with magic in them can get here!*

Belle darted into the tree.

A halo of golden light spread around her as she entered the cool mystery. The roots had formed an intricate, wall-like passage through the contorted trunk. She moved through the narrow passageway between the thick roots and the trunk into a stone cave.

Her heart gave a panicked thud when she heard the barking and the voices from outside, closer and clearer now.

Candle light danced across the small interior. The stolen jewellery box lay on a bed of dried grass and leaves. "Clara, it's me."

Barking burst out even closer. "There! Look! A tunnel through the hedge. She must have crawled through there!"

Belle grabbed the box without opening it. She quickly crept out of the cave and back around between the roots and the trunk. Her heart fluttered like a fairy trapped in a cage.

She crouched down to get under the roots and stepped out of the tree's belly.

Loud scrambling to her left revealed a dog's snarling muzzle poking out of the tunnel.

"It's her!" roared a voice. "The dogs have found her."

Belle turned on her heel, blew the candle out before dropping it, and sprinted the other way. She skipped up a haphazard set of steps formed by jagged rocks.

"Hey! You get over here, you scoundrel!" a man roared behind her. More insults boomed after her. Claws scratched on the rocks and an ear-splitting explosion deafened her momentarily.

"What are you doing, Frank? That's a child!" one man shouted.

"I don't care. They must not escape, you idiot!"

They want to kill me! Belle thought and scampered further up the rocky hill. Only being able to use one hand due to Clara's box in the other made navigating the sharp rocks difficult.

Another explosion and more hysterical barking.

The other side of the hill gently sloped down into another spread of woods.

She made it down and vanished into the darkness. Belle ran through the trees. Her bare feet slipped along the slimy leaves but she never looked back. "Clara," she said through her burning breath. "Clara, everything will be fine. I swear."

* * *

How long she ran until she reached the town of Châteauroux, Belle had no idea. What was clear was that her legs ached and her shoulder was on fire. It must have been a considerable amount of time because the moon had faded and hints of day appeared on the horizon. But she wasn't tired. The trees slowly gave way to farmland and soon the steeples and chimneys of the small town emerged out of the horizon.

She made it to the train station. Morning had chilled the air and only a few people waited up on the platform. Belle wanted to sit on the steel bench beside the tracks to rest her aching feet but decided against it. It was too open and maybe the men from the *château* were still looking for her.

When the ticket booth opened, a gentleman with a narrow face seated himself at the booth window. Belle stepped up to the counter and rose onto her tiptoes.

He looked down at her, perplexed. "Excuse me, *demoiselle*. You are too young to purchase a ticket. Where's your mother?"

Belle placed Clara's box on the counter. Next to that, she put down four coins she had stolen weeks earlier. Belle reached into the bag and came out with a folded piece of paper. The letter. Mére's words.

The gentleman huffed. "I am busy, *demoiselle*," he said as he shook his head but unfolded the letter anyway.

She watched as the agitation on his face became suspicion then confusion, then, finally, expressionless. A twitch pulled at the corner of his lips and he glanced at her. He gave her a small smile. "Well, *demoiselle*, I am sorry to hear that. You are a very brave young woman. And, by the sound of your mother's eloquent words, also very special. I hope she gets well soon." He reached under his counter and then slid a small paper ticket toward her. "One ticket to Paris. The train arrives in an hour."

"*Merci beaucoup, monsieur.*"

When she reached for the ticket the gentleman kept his fingers on it. "What's in the box, *demoiselle*?"

Belle swallowed hard. "My friend I found in the forest."

"Ah, a bird. I myself have birds at home. They tend to fall out of their nests this time of year. Unfortunately, the mothers are forced to abandon them once that happens. So, you are doing a good thing, *demoiselle*. What kind of bird is it?"

Belle stared at the gentleman. "A magic one."

He gave her a smile. "Of course. *Bon voyage, demoiselle.*"

* * *

The men from the *château* and the barking dogs did arrive at the train station. Belle watched them through the large train window just as they stormed onto the platform but the train was already pulling away. They didn't see her, but one of the dog's ears pricked up and the beast let out a hysterical fit of barking.

Belle sunk into her seat. After a long while, when the buildings gave way to the farms and the farms gave way to the forests, Belle took some cherries out of the bag and placed them on the empty seat next to her. Clara's box lay on her lap. Before she opened it, she glanced around the carriage. Barely anyone had boarded the train. Except for an old lady two seats in front of her and a young soldier further up, Belle's carriage was empty.

"I'm going to open the box, Clara. Mind your little eyes. The light will be bright."

She unclasped the lid and opened the box.

"Good morning, Clara."

* * *

A loud, bustling noise. People speaking. Belle's eyes drifted open. Sleep still draped her senses. Her forehead was squashed against the glass. The train had come to a stop. Streams of people passed by the window in all directions. She sat up with a gasp and her heart kicked into a gallop. *Where am I? Clara?*

The box lay on her lap, clasped shut. Belle breathed a sigh of relief. Her heart rate eased but as soon as she read the sign hanging from a platform post, her heart began its gallop once again. But this time it was excitement that quickened her pulse and not fear.

"*Bir-Hakeim*," Belle whispered the name of the station with a smile. How often had she seen that exact sign as a child when Mére and her had made excursions to Bordeaux?

"We're in Paris, Clara. I made it back."

Belle disembarked from the train, navigated her way through the crowds and up the stairs. She walked out of the station and stepped onto the sidewalk of *port de Stuffen* street. Although Belle's memory of the area was a fragmented picture, she recognized everything from Mére's descriptions in her letter.

Automobiles of all shapes and sizes chugged this way and that, couples walked hand in hand, bistros and cafés were alive with guests enjoying croissants and reading papers.

Belle took a moment to get her sense of direction and finally set her shoulders back and walked. She hurried by the bistros on her right, gazing at the glittering river Seine on her left. When she came to the *pont d'léna* bridge and looked to her right, Belle froze as joy washed over her.

There it was, ascending into the blue sky, standing over the city like God.

La tour Eiffel. Not a week went by that Belle and her Mére did not come here to read or ride on the carousel. This was Belle's favorite place in the world.

"Oh, Clara," Belle whispered. "How I wish you could see it." It was too risky to open the box with all these crowds. But soon.

Belle turned and crossed the *pont d'léna.* "We're almost home, Clara. Only a little way further."

As Belle and Clara walked over the river Seine, her anticipation grew. And her worry. How ill her Mére had been . . . that, Belle remembered. Tears had run down Mére's pale cheeks when the men in the black automobile had arrived to take Belle away.

"Your mother is no longer fit enough to take care of a child, demoiselle," the man in the black hat had said. *"This is not a fairy tale, this is real life. She is not getting better. Now let's go!"* Belle remembered the sound of the tires on the street as they crossed this very bridge. She remembered seeing *La tour Eiffel* against the grey winter skies. How empty Paris had been in that moment.

But now Belle had Clara, and Clara had promised to heal Mére.

Belle couldn't help but smile. Paris was the most beautiful city in the world, it was after all, *la Ville des Lumières* —The City of Lights. Belle glanced at her box. *And now we're adding another bright light to our beautiful city.*

They came to the end of the bridge and turned left onto *l'avenue de New York,* where mighty, lush oak trees lined the sidewalks. On sunny days like today the trees painted the street with pictures that swayed lazily. The apartments on the right faced the river.

Belle passed the first block of apartments and when she came to the second block, stopped at the first apartment. She looked up at a yellow brick building. On its small balcony with the cast-iron railing, two iron chairs still sat there, angled toward each other. Just the way Mére and Belle would always leave them.

Belle took a step toward the white door, but paused. The building blurred into a smudge of yellow and white. She raised her fingers to her eyes and felt the wetness streaming down her cheeks.

No, no. Not now. She climbed the first step then plopped down hard to sit on the second. Her breath came out in hitches. Tears flowed and Belle hugged

Clara's box to her breast. So many years of that dark place in the woods, so many years of beatings and harsh words and now, finally, here she was. Back at the very place where the most beautiful words she could remember were born. "Oh, *ma mére*. I made it, I made it back."

Belle didn't know how long she had been sitting there when a hand gently touched her shoulder. A sweet and pleasing fragrance embraced Belle. She looked up through her tears and saw a face gazing down at her. Mére's red scarf was around the blurry figure's neck.

"Mére!" Belle said in a teary gasp.

"Excuse me?" the lady said. "*Ça va, demoiselle?*" *Are you alright, young lady?*

Belle blinked, sniffed, and rubbed her eyes. She quickly stood up, glanced at the white door which now stood ajar and back at the tall woman with the curly blonde hair and the round, blue eyes. The red silk scarf and the light manner it was slung round her neck caught Belle's eye again. *Had Mére given this lady her scarf to wear? Mére always gave her things away to her friends.*

"Um," Belle stuttered. She wiped her eyes and straightened her posture the way Madame Desjardin always said a lady should.

Now that Belle was standing, the woman looked Belle up and down and her brow slightly creased.

"My name is Belle. Belle Beaulieu. Pleased to meet you." She held out her hand and immediately noticed its grubby appearance. Before she could pull it away the woman took it in her own and smiled.

The woman's lips parted ever-so-slightly as she stared at Belle. "Beaulieu?" she whispered, blinked and raised her chin as she regained composure. "My name is Delphine LeBlanc. How can I help you, Demoiselle Belle?"

"I would like to see Madame Floria Beaulieu, please. She is my mother," Belle said.

The lady tilted her head to the side, Belle's hand still clasped in the warmth of hers. Belle retracted her hand and pointed up at the yellow building. "This, um, this is our home."

She gazed at Belle for a long while. Belle shifted from foot to foot. The lady in Mére's scarf straightened. She was really tall. Her lips pressed together in a smile that seemed more unhappy than joyful. "May I ask where you have travelled from, Demoiselle Belle?"

Belle lowered her gaze. "Near Châteauroux. I came by train."

"Châteauroux? The orphanage. Oh, my! That is a long way indeed. Alone?" The alarm in her voice was soft but clear.

Belle nodded.

"I'm afraid Madame Beaulieu, well, she no longer lives here."

Belle blinked. She glanced at the yellow building, the small balcony where she and Mére always drank tea and recited tales, then back at Madame LeBlanc.

"Where does she live now?"

Another long look from the *madame* with Mére's red scarf. She turned around and walked back to the white door. When her hand closed around the handle, she paused and turned back to Belle who was standing on the step staring at her. "Come inside for a moment, Demoiselle Belle."

Belle did as she was told.

"Wait here a moment, please." Madame LeBlanc walked up a flight of stairs that once were wooden but were now carpeted cream.

Belle waited at the foot of the long staircase. She looked around, brewed in quietness. A stranger in her own dream. Gone were the little clay troll sculptures and the big potted plants with fairies wedged in the earth. Gone were all the candles and strange stones. The bright and beautifully-ugly paintings of trolls, wizards and gnomes were gone too. Gone was the big book shelf, the one that spanned the entire entrance from floor to ceiling. Gone were all their many bound tales and spells and recipes. Gone was Mére's sweet scent, too.

Now, everything was white and in place. No more cracks and flaky paint. Carpets covered wooden floors and, the dust motes that in the sunshine had glowed like fairies in a dream had vacated. This apartment was just an apartment.

Voices trickled down the staircase. Belle only heard fragments of a hushed conversation. *"There's a girl downstairs . . ."*

A cupboard door opened and closed and then footsteps. The tall lady appeared at the top of the stairs. She came down and held a coat out to Belle. "May I?"

Belle placed Clara's box down on the step, removed her bag and held her arms out.

Madame LaBlanc put the coat on her and buttoned it. "Perfect, *demoiselle*."

The two walked to the front door. "Let's go."

The tall lady stepped outside and turned around.

Belle didn't follow. "Are you taking me to *ma mére*?"

"Yes."

"Not back to the station?"

The lady took a deep breath and she gave Belle that smile again, the one that was more sad than happy. "Demoiselle Belle, we should go."

* * *

Belle read the words again.

'Dearly Departed Floria Beaulieu, daughter to Maximillian and Lucy Beaulieu, sister to Delphine Beaulieu and mother to Belle Beaulieu.'

She stared at the square stone in the ground.

'What use are our dreams and the words that paint them, if we cannot share them?'

Belle stood at the foot of her Mére's grave. For a moment, she simply stared at the cold stone in the ground. Some feet under that stone, her Mére's body lay. Maybe just a bunch of silent bones by now. Belle placed the Turkish delight at the foot of the grave stone along with a letter. Not her Mére's letter, but one that Belle had written. The letter described the ancient tree and the fairy with the broken wing that she had found lying there. These were her own words. Belle's words.

She looked up at Madame LeBlanc who clasped her hands in front of her.

"I came looking for you, Belle. I did. The woman there told me you had . . . you had died." Each word was spoken softly as if the lady was admitting a terrible secret. She unclasped her hands and retrieved a folded piece of paper from her coat pocket. Very delicately, she unfolded it and read it aloud.

Dear sister,

I know that you and I have not seen eye-to-eye. Can anyone blame us? I live most my life in the pages of fantasy, while you, my courageous sister, are on the battlefields, experiencing the harshest reality this life has to offer, saving the lives of our country's soldiers. We live in different worlds, you and I.

But I now have taken two steps into the real world. The first was with the birth of my little girl, Belle. I am now a mother and what a beautiful gift that has been. She is an astounding child with an imagination so vivid and miraculous that even I am left dumbfounded at times. I believe there is something so special in her. I have a strong feeling that she will succeed where I have failed—our family might have found France's next great author.

But, Delle, the next step into the real world I have taken is an ill one. I fear that I not only received our father's imagination but also the illness that he finally succumbed to. The reality that I have accepted, and no amount of fantasy has let me escape from, is that I am dying. Soon, I will no longer be fit to mother the most beautiful person in the world. There is no one left to take care of her. Except you, my Delle.

I write this to you without fantasy-filled words and ideas, as very real tears run down my cheeks. Don't let the authorities take my Belle. They will destroy the fragile flower she is. Please, Delphine,

*return to Paris and save my little girl. She will warm
your home and bring light into your world, the way
she has in mine. Please.*

Your sister, Floria.

Madame LeBlanc folded the letter up and closed
her hands around it. "Those were the last words I
received from your *mére*. Then when I saw you today, I
saw her. For a moment my sister was alive again."
Belle gazed at her mother's grave and then at her
aunt's face.
Delphine Beaulieu, now Delphine LeBlanc, who
wore Mére's scarf and had Mére's curly blonde hair
and the big blue eyes, was crying. But only a little.
Maybe that was how adults cried. Quietly and softly.
Belle was not an adult yet but she thought she must be
close because she cried in the same way.

* * *

Delphine Beaulieu's nose was red from the chill, as
were her eyes. She stood in front of the door at the top
of the stairs. This was Belle's room many years ago.
"Wait here, please, Belle." She pushed the door
open and stepped inside.
Belle waited. She held Clara's box. A faint
conversation drifted out from the room.
*"Her name is Belle. She's a little older than you.
Would you like to say hello, ma chérie?"*
"A girl?"
"Yes."
"Okay."

Footsteps on the carpet. Madame LeBlanc opened the door.

"Belle?"

"Yes, Madame LaBlanc."

"Would you like to say hello to your cousin? I think you two will get along well."

Belle nodded and Madame LeBlanc stepped to the side.

"I'll go make us something to eat, okay? You must be hungry."

Belle nodded.

"Um, Belle?"

Belle paused at the door and Madame LeBlanc ran her soft hands down Belle's head and cupped her face as if it were a fragile vase. She could not remember the last time she had felt such tenderness. "You are home now. Okay?"

Belle gave her aunt a nod and her heart warmed. "Home," she said.

"Our home," Aunt Delle said. "The place you belong."

A girl lay on the bed by the window. She lay in sunlight and it shone through the wisps of blonde hair that barely covered her head. Her skin was pasty and very pale. Tired eyes shifted over to Belle as she stepped up to the bed.

"*Bonjour*," Belle said.

The tired girl stared at her for a moment. "*Comment tu t'appelles*?" *Who are you?*

"My name is Belle," Belle said. She looked around a room that resembled a hospital room more than it did a girl's. White, bare of paintings and plants. And books.

Belle sat down in the chair beside the bed covered in white sheets.

"Are you tired?" asked Belle.

"Yes. A little. I'm always tired. Every day I feel a little more tired than the day before. The doctor says I am very sick."

Belle nodded.

"I'm Mélodie."

Belle looked at Mélodie and her smile touched her eyes. "Oh, that is such a beautiful name. A melody. A song."

Mélodie gazed at her with a frown.

"This used to be my room and when I went to sleep, *ma mére* would sing for me. This room was always filled with the joy of a melody. Like it is now."

Mélodie didn't respond. Her gaze drifted down at the box in Belle's hands.

"What's in there?"

Belle stood up and placed the box on Mélodie's waist. She took Mélodie's cool hands and placed them on Clara's box.

"Okay, Mélodie. Clara is a little shy but I think she will like you. Are you ready?"

Mélodie gave a nod. Belle unclasped the box. She slowly opened the lid.

Mélodie's lips parted and her eyes widened. When she smiled, her face absorbed the sunshine and filled not with colour, but with a golden glow.

———

Eddie Cantrell loves music as much as he loves writing. When the lights go out, he retreats to his small man-cave, turns on Alice In Chains or Soundgarden or anything that rocks, and so the writing begins. He is also involved with creating story-telling podcasts; a medium that combines his writing and music passions. His short stories, *A Grave Tale, Teeth* and *Blue Sandman* were published in anthologies by Dark Alley Press and Fairfield Scribes. *When To Now: A Time Travel Anthology*, which included his story, *Blue Sandman*, was featured on the Amazon Bestseller list. In an effort to keep improving his writing, he is an active member of Scribophile. Eddie and his wife live happily somewhere in the German countryside.

FOLD OF FIRE AND EARTH

ELIN KORUND

The London Ledger, July Edition, 1924

Magic in the Desert!

Move over King Tut! A new ancient wonder stands in the limelight. After years of searching, archeologists have finally located their first Djeeni monument. A mysterious civilization, the Djeen ruled the Nile Valley long before Egypt's pharaohs, but unlike the pharaohs who built monuments out of stone, the Djeen used spacetime itself.

That's right. These ancients found a way to conceal their sacred monuments inside pockets of space cut off from normal reality, and which can only be accessed by specific means.

The Belgian archeologists who made the discovery are the first to ever successfully locate and open one of these Djeeni 'vaults'. Inside, they reportedly found a dome-shaped room covered in ancient frescoes and a stone altar.

Researchers are still uncertain of the vault's purpose, though the presence of an altar suggests religious significance. It has been speculated that it served as a funerary chapel or tomb, but no sarcophagi or remains have been found within.

Historians and scientists alike are calling the Djeeni vault 'magical' as its existence cannot yet be explained by modern physics. Departments of 'Djeenology' are forming in universities all across Europe, as each nation seeks to be the first to unravel the mysteries of Djeeni technology.

CHAPTER ONE

Sophie Lancaster flinched as a passing camel let out a bellowing growl. Hurrying to get out of the grumpy beast's way, she nearly tripped over her own hiking boots before her young Berber escort, Jamelu, grabbed her arm and steadied her.

"*Attention!*" Jamelu cautioned for the fifth time that day, and for the fifth time she nodded apologetically. It was difficult to 'watch out' for everything going on in the chaos of the bazaar. A dozen shouting hawkers wove an impenetrable blanket of noise, and the dusty haze kicked up by the throngs of locals shuffling around her rivaled London's own fog for opaqueness.

Sophie leaned against a shady wall to get out of the traffic to tuck her unruly auburn curls back under her floppy straw hat. Three days of exploring Oran, and she still felt like a leaf swirled on the dizzying current of a stream.

No matter! She was in Africa *at last*, her clumsy feet standing on the continent which had given birth to such amazing ancient cultures. The bedtime stories Uncle Andrew once shared about his North African travels had filled her young mind with awe, and now that she was an Arcane Society graduate student, she was finally exploring it herself—a reality that filled her with both nervous jitters and excitement.

An impatient finger poked her hip. Jamelu frowned at her. Slight of build beneath his dark blue burnoose, he couldn't have been more than fourteen—just a boy— and yet his grandfather, one of the local chieftains or '*beys*', had tasked him with chaperoning her after learning that a foreign lady wandered Oran's streets alone.

"*Allons-y*?" he asked, no doubt hoping to get out of his tiresome escort duties early that day.

"*Non*," she answered and Jamelu sighed as they moved on. Even with his open disdain, Jamelu's company was preferable to following the Society tour group around all day. No doubt Professor Fiddlekey would berate her for playing hooky again, but she hadn't begged and bribed her way into a slot on this year's Africa Tour just to hear the same old tired lectures.

No, she had another purpose—a hope—which dimmed a little more with each new street she explored.

When the Djeeni vaults were first created, they'd dotted the shores of the Nile River, but millennia of slow spacial drift on the Earth's magnetic currents had scattered them from Libya to Morocco. Still, no vaults had ever been found this far north on the Algerian coast, and most Djeenologists had even stopped looking here, since all the maps which had been drawn from the existing data, showed the currents flowing further south.

However, her Uncle Andrew had believed the maps were wrong, or at best incomplete. Why else had no one located the Vault of Djamuu yet? There had to be more vaults—more data points—they were missing. And so she searched, though even if her late uncle was right, finding a vault in Oran had always been a long shot.

Hunger gnawed at Sophie's stomach.

"Are you hungry?" she asked Jamelu in English. The boy just wrinkled his brow and stared. He didn't speak English, and she only knew a smattering of French. Languages had always been difficult for her, their grammar rules so arbitrary and illogical. So unlike the comforting rigidity of mathematics. It was a small miracle that she'd become decent at reading Djeeni script. Then again, few had taught with such steady patience as her uncle.

Sophie mimicked biting and chewing food. At this, her young bodyguard shrugged with indifference, but she knew from experience this meant yes. She'd managed to bribe a better mood out of him the day before with some *harissa* and other sticky sweets. Perhaps she could do it again.

They moved onward through the bazaar, past stalls displaying bright ceramics, fluttering scarfs, and baskets of fragrant spices. She'd just spotted a vendor selling baked goods, when the amber beads of her dowsing necklace thrummed against her skin like silent alarm bells.

Her breath caught. The special, copper-inlaid beads only reacted when a vault was close by. She'd couldn't believe it. She'd actually found a vault in Oran!

With a full turn to pinpoint the direction of the energy, she set off at a pace which had Jamelu struggling to keep up. The energy signal led toward the sea, just as Uncle Andrew had predicted, and Sophie managed a grin despite the way her face twitched at each of the necklace's stinging electric shocks.

Depending on which magnetic current they rode, vaults could drift anywhere from five to fifty meters a year. This vault must have wandered along the floor of the Mediterranean for centuries, resurfacing only recently.

With one last painful snap, the necklace went silent, and Sophie stopped in a narrow, deserted alley. The vault was here somewhere.

Briefly, she considered fetching Professor Fiddlekey and the others before proceeding, but she'd come this far without their help. Opening this vault herself was a chance to prove her competence as a Djeenologist. Besides, Fiddlekey wouldn't believe she'd found a vault here unless she returned with physical proof.

Sophie knelt and unslung the bulky leather satchel that rested against her hip. From it, she took out her dowsing kit: a pair of red amber wands bundled in rabbit fur, and two electrically-insulated gloves that might've been mistaken for falconry gauntlets.

"Non!" Jamelu caught her arm. Alarm widened his eyes. *"N'invoque pas les talents surnaturels des Djeenis."*

Sophie blinked, then gave a startled laugh. She'd heard many locals still feared the Djeen, believing them to be vengeful desert ghosts who snatched away any who offended them or stole their treasures.

"*Oui*, Djeeni magic," she replied, pulling her arm free. Jamelu smoldered but said nothing more. He lacked any real authority over her and they both knew it. Still, he backed several paces away with genuine worry on his face, and Sophie realized that were it not for his grandfather's command, he might've bolted altogether.

"*Pardon*," she apologized. She shouldn't have laughed at him, and knew all too well that hateful sense of disregard. "You'll be okay," she promised as she pulled on her gauntlets. Then, she rubbed the amber wands against the rabbit fur to charge them.

Djeenology students were taught to picture a vault like a flower bud with petals made of spacetime folded around it, gathering at the bud's pointed tip. That gathering point was the keyhole. Find it, and you could open the flower.

Waving her wands back and forth in a slow, grid-like pattern, Sophie searched the alley for the keyhole. A few passing locals stopped to stare. Sophie was used to getting looks. Proper English ladies didn't dirty their clothes combing beaches for amber, or building electrical devices in workshops. They were supposed to get married, have children, and then sit around all day devouring tea cakes and gossip. She'd never understood what was so proper about that.

Jamelu noticed the gawkers and waved his curved silver dagger at them with a spray of angry words. They hurried off and Sophie smiled. At least there were some advantages to having a babysitter.

As Sophie moved to the other side of the alley to continue her slow search, a glowing burst of electric current arched between her wands. It vanished almost before she had time to flinch, like lightning swirling into an invisible whirlpool.

The keyhole. Now for the key.

Sophie took out her gyroplant, a portable self-contained generator that resembled a miniature gramophone, only instead of a trumpet-shaped speaker, it sported an adjustable copper antenna.

Opening a vault—and keeping it open—required a steady flow of electricity, and this particular gyroplant was of her own design, far smaller and lighter than the field generators lugged around by the Society on expeditions.

Theoretically it was perfect . . . but she'd never actually tried it on a vault before. There simply weren't any in Britain to practice with.

Feeling the same jitters as before an exam, Sophie placed the gyroplant on the ground and positioned the crystal-tipped end of the antenna over the keyhole. Then, she grasped the gyroplant's handle and cranked, spinning the magnetically-suspended, near-frictionless gears inside faster and faster.

Electricity hummed up the antenna and into the keyhole. A halo of darkness formed around the antenna's crystal tip, fuzzy-edged and growing as the electric current peeled back the fabric of reality concealing the vault.

It was working! Sophie had studied newsreel footage and photographs, but this was the first time she'd seen a vault open in person. Watching spacetime distort and peel back to create a portal felt like peering behind the stage curtain at the strange rules which governed the universe itself. She wanted so badly to understand them, to solve the mystery, and to prove that her uncle had been right.

Jamelu gasped. He wore the expression of someone in the path of a charging elephant or train, and yet shakily held his ground.

"Safe . . . um, *non dangereux*," she assured him with a smile. It did little good.

The portal expanded to roughly three meters in diameter before stabilizing. Wrapped in awe, Sophie realized she'd continued cranking the gyroplant long after she needed to. Spun up, it would run on its own for a good hour.

She stood and peered through the portal. A short flight of stone steps led down to a dirt floor. Little else was visible without more light.

She turned to Jamelu and pointed at the gyroplant. "Um . . . *garde* this?" If anyone disturbed it while she was in the vault and cut off the flow of electricity, she could be trapped inside.

Jamelu nodded, relief flooding his posture. No doubt he was glad to keep away from her evil Djeeni magic.

Small metal lighter in hand, Sophie took a deep breath and strode past the gyroplant into the vault. Her *first* vault. Excitement pounding in her chest, she almost skipped down the stairs like a giddy school girl.

The air inside was cool and surprisingly pleasant, smelling of incense and fresh straw. She raised the lighter's soft orange flame to the domed walls. Brilliant frescoes in blue, green and orange stretched upward into cavernous shadows, as rich and pristine as if they'd been painted yesterday. It was believed that time passed more slowly within the vaults, cut loose from the rest of the world not just in the three spacial dimensions, but in the fourth dimension of time as well.

The glimmer of metal further in caught Sophie's eye. Waist-high stone pillars led toward the center of the vault, each topped with an oil lamp. *Golden* oil lamps.

Sophie lit the nearest one, filling the room with a brighter glow. Most of the vaults discovered so far had been vandalized by ancient thieves, and stripped of anything valuable. Did the presence of these lamps mean this was an unlooted vault?

Sophie hurried down the row of lamps to the center of the room. There, she found the altar. Humbly displayed on its stone slab was a polished rock crystal sphere the size of a billiard ball. A sun eye.

Believed to be used as part of some sun-worshipping ceremony, nearly every vault found so far contained one of these spheres, but they were always knocked from their ornate glass pedestals onto the ground, or even shattered by desecrating thieves.

But this one remained just as the Djeen had left it, on display, undamaged and . . . opaque?

Frowning, Sophie lit another oil lamp and moved in for a closer look. 'Rock crystal' was simply the name given to unflawed quartz—chunks of the mineral so pure, they were as transparent as glass itself—a geologic rarity which the Djeen had clearly valued. But this sun eye had a foggy, flawed appearance, as if carved from inferior material. An odd choice for a sacred object.

. . . And yet there was something about the milky flaws that didn't seem natural. The foggy web of tiny cracks and creases within the stone were evenly spaced and angled, almost like intentional folds.

Sophie marveled at the complexity of the intricate pattern. Was this another demonstration of the Djeen's ability to manipulate matter? But why go to the trouble of changing the internal structure of this quartz, and how did they do it?

Sophie started to reach for the sun eye, but stopped short.

Dust motes swirling in the air around it were acting strangely . . . twitching and polarizing, as if caught in a static electric field.

She blinked in surprise. Was the sun eye electrically-charged like a battery? Quartz *was* piezoelectric—able to generate a charge when physically stressed or compressed. That might explain the orderly flaws in the stone, and the insulating glass pedestal it rested on would prevent it from releasing that charge.

To be safe, Sophie put one of her bulky protective gauntlets back on. She needed to show this thrilling find to Fiddlekey. Not only would it prove she'd found a vault, but she wanted to test her battery theory in a controlled setting with witnesses. If she was right, the discovery might earn her a little respect from the crusty old men on the Arcane Society's governing board.

"*Mademoiselle!*" Jamelu shrieked.

Sophie turned. Just beyond the portal, she saw Jamelu draw his knife to meet an attacker. The man, his face concealed by the *shemagh* wrapped around it, was almost twice Jamelu's size, and as they wrestled for control of the knife, was clearly going to win.

Fear caught in Sophie's throat, and not just for Jamelu. If they bumped the gyroplant . . .

Sun eye still clutched in her gloved hand, Sophie raced for the portal. She dropped the lighter in her other hand and rummaged in her satchel for her revolver. She had to help Jamelu. She had to get out of the vault.

She was on the steps when Jamelu was shoved down through the portal at her. Sophie's arms came up in defense as they collided and Jamelu fell against her gloved hand holding the crystal sphere. There was a loud snapping sound, like that made by static electricity arcing through the air. Jamelu went rigid, then passed out on top of her.

Pinned beneath his weight at the bottom of the stairs, Sophie looked up. Their attacker stood at the portal, gazing down at them in triumph, before his attention turned to the gyroplant. He drew back a leg to kick it.

No! Sophie raised her revolver and fired several shots in blind succession. The man let out a cry, stumbled back, and fled from view.

Sophie managed to push Jamelu off her and sit up. The boy was still breathing, still had a pulse. A sigh of relief rattled out of her lungs.

"Jamelu?" She patted his cheek gently. "Wake up."

Jamelu's eyelids flickered, then opened. He gasped and sat up, looking around in terror.

"You're okay—*tout bien*," she assured, but he slapped her hands away and rose. Babbling angrily, he staggered up the steps and fled.

Dumbfounded, Sophie watched him go before crawling out of the vault herself. She sat beside the gyroplant, limbs suddenly weak, thoughts scattered by shock. A crowd gathered, but she barely noticed them even as the shrill whistles of police neared.

Her gaze dropped to the sun eye still clutched in her glove. The milky sphere had gone clear as glass.

* * *

Sophie focused on the paper square in her hands, measuring each fold visually before committing the crease. Slowly, she reshaped the two-dimensional square into an origami snail.

She always kept paper in her satchel. Folding it helped focus her anxious mind—something she desperately needed now. Her hands no longer shook, but she still smelled the gunpowder on them, still felt the slap of the recoil. Uncle Andrew had taught her how to shoot, but this was the first time she'd used a weapon in self defense. The moment was burned into memory and dampened the thrill of her discovery.

Professor Fiddlekey paced in front of the ornate Louis XVI armchair she sat in, traversing the length of his hotel suite in great angry strides. His white mustache bristled as he puffed back and forth like a slightly-rotund tea kettle building up steam for a good howl.

Finally he boiled over and spun on his heel to face her. "Quit worrying at that scrap of paper! Have you any idea the trouble you'd be in if you'd killed that man?"

Sophie's gaze snapped up from the paper snail, her own anger rising in spite of efforts to remain calm. "Oh, I'm *terribly* sorry, Professor. You're right: I should've let him *murder* us in cold blood."

Fiddlekey shook his head. "This is no trifling matter, Miss Sophia."

"Indeed not, and I resent the implication that I'm somehow to blame for it."

"You left the safety of the tour group. *Again.*"

"I had Jamelu with me," she countered, but felt the strength slip from her argument. Jamelu had mostly been for show and they both knew it.

"And what if Jamelu had been hurt, or worse?" asked Fiddlekey. "Do you think his grandfather would've supported our continued presence here? My entire annual curriculum could've been jeopardized."

Sophie's gaze dropped to the Persian rug at her feet. She didn't care one iota about his curriculum, but she felt bad about Jamelu. She'd told him it was safe, and not only had they been attacked, but it seemed her battery theory was correct and he'd been shocked by that sun eye. He still hadn't come back, and she felt terrible about the whole ordeal.

"Have they found the man who attacked us yet?" she asked.

"No." Fiddlekey sighed wearily and dropped onto the striped divan across from her.

Sophie began unfolding her origami snail. The motive for the attack still baffled her. Did the locals really fear 'Djeeni magic' enough to kill over it?

. . . Could there actually be some truth to the Order of Djamuu? An occult mob rumored to go around murdering Djeenologists, Sophie had believed the

Order to be nothing more than wild fiction, fit only for pulp magazines and penny dreadfuls. Now, uncertainty lingered.

A knock at the door interrupted her thoughts.

"Go away!" Fiddlekey shouted.

"*Senhor* Fiddlekey," a muffled voice replied. "It is most urgent."

Sophie recognized the accented voice of Mendoça, the Portuguese Djeenologist who'd introduced himself on the docks. Mendoça had offered his local expertise in exchange for the chance to tour with England's prestigious Arcane Society. Initially Fiddlekey had shooed him away, but like a hungry stray, Mendoça had followed the group, persisting until Fiddlekey relented.

Once again Mendoça stubbornly persisted until a furious Fiddlekey rose and threw open the door. "Have you no concept of privacy?" he bellowed.

Mendoça smiled meekly. His faded green trousers and tattered yellow sun scarf made him look like a traveler fresh from the desert, as did his rough beard and shaggy curls.

"Apologies," Mendoça dipped in contrition, "but I fear nothing is private here. Already Oran buzzes with word of the discovery."

"Well that's bloody perfect," Fiddlekey grumbled. "In a week, there'll be more Djeenologists here than seagulls." He turned to the coat rack beside the door and retrieved his jacket. "I must contact the proper authorities immediately and claim this find for the Society."

Sophie jumped to her feet. "But it's *my* find!"

Fiddlekey pulled on his coat with a groan. "Think, Sophie. The Algerian government doesn't grant excavation licenses to just anyone—and certainly not to rogue individuals who engage in gun battles on their streets."

"That's unfair, and you know it!" she shouted, before recoiling in surprise at the loudness of her own voice. She couldn't remember being so angry before. No, that wasn't true. She'd been this angry once, long ago, the day death had stolen her parents.

Fiddlekey regarded her calmly, the edges of his mouth turned downward in that pained look headmasters so often gave to students who failed the simplest test.

"Listen to yourself," he scolded softly. "You think I don't know the real reason you came? You're determined to validate your uncle's theories, and that emotional investment is clouding your judgment. Hysteria has no place in science, and I refuse to be responsible for your wellbeing while pursuing these misguided efforts."

"You needn't concern yourself," she shot back.

Fiddlekey tugged on his lapels to tidy their drape. "I won't. Because I'm sending you back to England on the next available ship."

Sophie stared in shock. "You can't. I helped fund this year's trip with my inheritance!"

"If you wish to remain in the Society, you'll do as you're told."

Fiddlekey opened the door and marched out, leaving Sophie dumbstruck, and Mendoça looking embarrassed at witnessing their argument.

"Apologies," he offered with sympathy.

"Why? It's not your fault." Sophie tried to sound brave, to hide how crushed she was, but as tears threatened she turned away. She'd worked so hard to get here, and now it was all being taken away!

"If I may say, *Senhora*, you impress me." The warmth in Mendoça's tone suggested he actually meant it. "To find a vault here, you have good instincts."

Sophie shook her head. "I was only testing one of my uncle's theories." Unlike others, she would not steal credit, not even from the dead.

Mendoça gave a jovial chuckle. "Well, if your uncle had other theories, I would certainly like to hear them."

Sophie blinked. Of course! She'd been so wrapped up in the day's drama, that she'd forgotten the implications of her find. The maps of the Sahara's magnetic currents were wrong. This new vault proved it. It also provided a crucial new data point for accurately remapping the currents.

They may have stolen this new vault away from her, but she wouldn't let anyone steal her uncle's legacy. She had to act on this information now, before any others did.

Sophie spun to face the Portuguese Djeenologist. "Mr. Mendoça, you offered your services to the members of our tour group, did you not? Tell me, how quickly could you arrange transport to the Ahaggar Mountains?"

Precise calculations would take time, but the new map data placed the fabled vault somewhere in that region.

Mendoça's brow wrinkled with confusion. "This very day, *Senhora*. But why?"

Unable to contain her excitement, she smiled broadly. "How would you like to help me find the Vault of Djamuu?"

Slowly, Mendoça understood her intention and matched her grin.

"I would like that very much."

The Parisian Gazette, Spring 1929

Al Kev Expedition Vanishes!

Members of a prestigious international research team have disappeared in the eastern Sahara. Led by the renowned Dr. Gustaf Breunner, the team had been in search of the priceless Vault of Djamuu, or 'Vault of Kings' as it's commonly translated.

Mentioned in the Khunenmu Tablet—the artifact which provided instructions on how to open Djeeni vaults—the Vault of Kings is believed to contain royal artifacts of tremendous significance and Breunner's expedition was the latest of many attempts to locate it.

Contact with Breunner's expedition was lost in December, after one final communiqué arrived in Tunisia with a supply caravan. The note claimed the team had detected a vault and were close to locating its entrance.

In January, search parties recovered the bodies of researchers Jarl Frederich and Paolo Caveizel. Both had been shot in the back. No other members of the expedition have been found.

CHAPTER TWO

If anyone ever asked Sophie what riding a camel was like, she would compare it to trying to sit atop one of those wobbly fruit gelatins they served at fancy teas. Days into the journey, her legs ached from the effort of trying to keep from sliding off the beast.

And the sand! Even wrapped in layers of protective linen and cotton, her chapped skin burned wherever the blowing grit worked its way in. She couldn't decide which hurt more: her cracked lips or cramped knees.

The only pleasant distraction she found was in imagining the look on Fiddlekey's face when he discovered she'd left Oran, but not on the boat. Oh, she would've liked to see the old tea kettle sputter over that one!

On the other hand, she *was* risking what little academic standing she had on this hasty endeavor. If she failed to find the Vault of Djamuu with her newly-revised map, she was unlikely to get another chance. Certainly, the Society would never help her again, and Mendoça's support might even dry up if this proved a wild goose chase.

Her fingers rose to the copper and amber beads circling her neck, rubbing them to produce little snapping sparks between her fingertips. The dowsing necklace was a cherished gift from her late uncle, and she prayed that it would guide her to success for both their sakes.

"Is all good, *Senhora*?" Mendoça asked, steering his camel alongside hers. "You look troubled."

"It's just the heat," she answered.

Mendoça nodded, or perhaps only bobbed with the camel's gait. "You will get used to it."

"You've lived in Africa a while?"

"*Sim.*" He smiled. "A long time."

"Then you would know if there's any truth to the Order of Djamuu."

Mendoça shook his head. "There is no Order of Djamuu, no bands of zealots running around murdering Djeenologists."

"But so many have gone missing since Al Kev."

"Because of bandits or bad choices. Most Djeenologists are pipe-smoking old men who have never journeyed farther than the nearest café. They have no survival skills, and the dunes bury their bodies. But no one calls them fools. Instead, they were *great men*," Mendoça said, stretching his arms as if giving a passionate speech, "and some evil must have befallen them!" He laughed and put his arms down with a shrug. "So the Order is invented to take the blame." He looked at her, and quickly added, "But I do not consider *you* this sort of Djeenologist."

"Naturally." Sophie smiled. "I don't smoke a pipe."

While Mendoça's reasoning made sense, Sophie's uneasiness refused to be comforted. She'd never thought herself prone to paranoia but out here, in this vast ocean of sand, she felt vulnerable to whatever dangers lurked in its expanse. It still bothered her how quickly she'd been attacked in Oran. Surely murderous thieves didn't linger on every street corner. Had that man been following her and Jamelu?

She glanced over her shoulder. Did someone follow now?

* * *

The wheezing melody of a lute drifted through the oasis like smoke from the campfires. Stars slowly woke in the darkening twilight above as Sophie listened and folded paper beside her small fire.

Nearly a month had passed since leaving Oran. Callouses now toughened her skin, and like a sailor on the high seas, she'd adjusted to the rocking gait of her perpetually-grumpy camel. She could even pitch her little personal tent in under six minutes, and prepare the evening rations of flat bread and boiled jerky with little effort.

Mendoça returned from visiting the camel drivers who always made a separate camp away from theirs.

"Our guides say we will reach the Ahaggar in two days." He sat down on the little rug opposite hers and poured himself a cup of tea from the long-spouted kettle nestled in the fire's red coals.

"Why do they still avoid us?" Sophie asked. Even during the day, the camel drivers kept their distance, traveling ahead of them. "Do they dislike foreigners that much?"

"No." Mendoça blew on his tea. "It is because of the Djeeni treasure. They fear we shall find what we seek."

"The treasure?"

"The Djeen. The legends here are old and many . . . stories about unlucky travelers stumbling into vaults, never to be seen again."

Sophie frowned. "I don't see how that's possible." Vaults didn't just open without a proper charge . . . though perhaps an electrical storm might do it.

Mendoça shrugged. "Who can say? But in their minds, the Djeen still live, roaming the desert as fiery ghosts, leading trespassers astray."

Mendoça pointed to the half-finished origami giraffe in her hands. "Why do you do that?" he asked.

"It reminds me never to lose hope," she answered. Puzzlement rippled across Mendoça's face.

"I was only seven when my parents died," she explained. "I was sent to my uncle in Scotland. It was cold there, and rained almost as often as I cried. But even in that miserable state, my uncle sat with me in the attic and crafted little dolls and animals out of old newsprint. It was like watching a magician conjure toys from nothing. In those moments I forgot my grief and begged to learn his tricks."

Sophie finished her giraffe and planted it in the sand beside her rug. "Folding reminds me of the possibilities. That even when hopeless and grieving in the dark, reality can be reshaped into something better."

Mendoça's expression softened. "Again, you impress me, *Senhora*. And not just because you are the first female Djeenologist I have met."

Sophie scoffed and fetched another square from her satchel. "It took six years of begging and the outright bribe of funding this year's tour before the Society let me come. It's not surprising I'm the first you've met."

Mendoça gave her an impish smile. "As you say, reality can be reshaped. Perhaps one day, men will beg you for *permissão*. Tell me, what do you think is in the Vault of Djamuu?"

"The past, of course," she answered, then added quickly, "and the future."

Again Mendoça's brow scrunched in puzzlement at her strange answer and she laughed.

"It's just that we still know so little about the Djeen. The vaults we've found contain so few artifacts. We don't even have a dynastic timeline for them like we do for the Egyptians because they just called all their rulers 'Djamuu', even when the frescoes clearly depict different rulers, even female ones."

Mendoça nodded. "It is troubling how little is left of their empire. Just the vaults, it seems."

"And what a maddening mystery they are!" Sophie said, almost crumpling the next origami animal she worked at. She was getting too excited again and forced herself to relax with slow breaths.

Her thoughts drifted to the hours she and Uncle Andrew used to spend sipping tea while rain spattered the windows, dreaming about the wonders humanity might perform if they only understood Djeeni technology. Perhaps bubbles of spacetime could be used to move goods and passengers safely and swiftly along magnetic railways. Or serve as leak-proof vehicles for exploring deep under the ocean, or even float explorers to the moon!

Like all the shapes she fashioned from her paper squares, the possibilities might be endless. Vault technology could reshape the world, and just maybe, she'd have a hand in that.

* * *

The cry of a night bird woke Sophie with a start. The moon had risen, its light glowing pale through the canvas weave of her little tent. She lay there, staring up at the glow. The nearer they came to their destination, the more elusive sleep grew, her mind busy with worry over the accuracy of her map, of potential retaliation by the Society, and over the many missing expeditions before her. She couldn't let the doubts win, not when she'd come so far, but even her origami animals did little to calm her nerves now.

A shadow moved across her tent. The outline of a human figure. Groggy from sleep, she was slow to react when the flap of her tent opened. The figure lunged inside, a dagger raised against the moonlight.

Sophie shrieked, her arms raising in defense. The dagger's thrust deflected off her left forearm with a burning slice across it. She managed to grab her attacker's wrist and trap the dagger against the ground as she screamed for help. Her attacker wasn't big, and their strength was matched as they struggled for control of the blade.

Mendoça burst in, snatched her attacker by the shoulders, and yanked him backward out of the tent. The sounds of a skirmish followed outside.

Hands shaking, Sophie found her revolver and staggered through the flap, but the fight was over by then. Mendoça and all three camel drivers held her attacker belly-down in the sand, arms pinned behind him.

Mendoça came to her, inspected the warm trickle of blood down her arm, and asked something, but she didn't hear the words. An oil lamp had been brought, and in its hazy yellow glow she stared at her attacker's face. It was Jamelu.

<u>Revue Électrique, December 1927</u>

Moods were heated at this year's Solvay Conference, where the world's top scientists continued to debate the viability of a new field of study called 'quantum mechanics', and how it might explain the existence of Djeeni vaults.

Niels Bohr insisted their existence must be related to the uncertain nature of quantum states, claiming that vaults both exist, and do not exist at the same time. Albert Einstein dismissed this explanation, believing the answer lay in some unexplored aspect of electro-magnetism.

Marie Curie theorized that an undiscovered element might be responsible for their magical, math-breaking creation, but members of the gallery laughed at this idea, calling it alchemy, not science.

CHAPTER THREE

An hour before dawn, the camel driver guarding Jamelu finally fell asleep. Sophie watched from behind one of the dozing camels awhile longer to make sure.

Ever since that dreadful night, her insomnia had worsened. Why had Jamelu come all this way to attack her? It made no sense, and Mendoça had refused to let her near Jamelu, saying the child was mad and babbled incoherently whenever questioned. They planned to leave him in Tazrouk, a small settlement on the edge of the Ahaggar where locals could hold him until the authorities arrived.

Sophie needed answers before then. She would never sleep again without them.

They'd tied Jamelu to one of the stakes used for securing the camels at night, and he sat with his back against it, arms bound behind.

Sophie crept toward him, her boots silent in the soft sand. Unlike his guard, Jamelu sat awake and glared as she approached. She knelt in front of him, careful to stay just out of reach in case he somehow broke free. She also had her satchel and the revolver within, but she didn't want to think about needing it.

"*Je suis désolée,*" she whispered in apology, rubbing her arms against the chill night breeze. The knife wound on her forearm still ached. It was shallow, but long enough that it had required stitching. The skin stung whenever she flexed it.

His expression murderous, Jamelu spat on the ground between them and muttered in a language she didn't understand. Berber, she assumed.

"*En français?*" she asked. Had he forgotten it was the only common language between them?

Jamelu repeated his gibbering and struggled against his ropes. Despair sank through Sophie's gut. Mendoça was right—this wasn't the same boy she'd known in Oran.

She'd heard of people struck by lightning sometimes changing, their personalities completely different than before. Sometimes even their memories. Had that happened when Jamelu was shocked by the sun eye? Realizing she might be to blame stung far more than the gash on her arm.

She wanted to communicate so badly, but how? Desperate, she smoothed the sand in front of him and began to write out an apology with her finger. Perhaps the shock had damaged Jamelu's ability to speak French, but he could still read it.

She was only half-finished when Jamelu swept a foot across the sand, erasing her efforts, and then clumsily wrote with his toe, *"Death to Djamuu'.*

In Djeeni script.

Sophie's mouth fell open. The Jamelu she'd known hated all things Djeeni, so how could he now write their language? It was impossible, and yet here it was— much like the vaults themselves. But if this impossibility let them communicate . . .

'Why did you attack me?' she wrote in the sand.

Jamelu read, then responded, *'You serve Djamuu, vile priest.'*

Sophie paused. What was he talking about? *'I am not a priest.'*

Jamelu snorted. *'You wield the amber and quartz. You travel with Utheel.'*

'Utheel?'

"He means me," Mendoça said. Sophie spun to find him standing behind her along with the camel drivers. Footsteps silenced by the sand, she hadn't heard them approach.

Mendoça wore a strange smirk that made Sophie's neck hairs raise. Something wasn't right. Fear guided her hand into her satchel for the revolver, but the camel drivers pounced, grabbing and pinning her arms before she could find it.

"What is this?" Sophie demanded. "Let go of me!"

Mendoça sighed. "I'd hoped you would not discover this yet."

"That you're a double-crossing scoundrel?" she said, struggling in vain against her captors.

Mendoça smiled. "That I am Utheel, high priest of Djamuu the Ever-Rising." He gestured at the camel drivers. "And these are my fellow priests. Those who survived, at least."

Sophie shook her head. "You're making even less sense than Jamelu!"

"That is not Jamelu," Mendoça said, walking around her to face the boy. Jamelu spat at his feet and Mendoça answered the insult with a kick to the boy's ribs.

"His name is Shoht," Mendoça continued, "and he is a traitor. Millenia ago, this rebel and his followers tried to destroy us, but his failure will be complete when Djamuu is resurrected."

Resurrected. Sophie blinked as the pieces tumbled horribly into place.

"'Djamuu' isn't the Djeeni word for 'ruler' is it? It's the name of one ruler, living over and over again in different bodies."

She saw it now. The sun eyes weren't batteries, but they *were* storage devices. The meticulous folds she'd seen within the quartz sphere had been data, compressed and ordered like in the folds of a brain. The Djeen hadn't just tucked away pockets of space, they'd learned how to tuck minds away as well.

Mendoça crouched down to her level. "This is why I like you. Few are so quick to understand." He took away her satchel and rummaged through it. "I was

worried you might recognize my compatriots, so I
instructed them to keep their distance."

He motioned for the nearest camel driver to remove
the *shemagh* covering his face.

Sophie gasped as she recognized Gustaf Breunner,
leader of the lost Al Kev expedition. After its
disappearance, photos of him had been in the London
papers for months.

"You're alive," she whispered in awe.

"No." Mendoça shook his head. "Breunner is dead.
Those who used to own these bodies are gone. We now
live in them."

Sophie began to feel dizzy from processing it all.
"But how?"

"Breunner went searching for the Vault of Djamuu,
but found our vault instead. We too, were hidden away
to serve Djamuu upon his return. Thankfully, Shoht's
rebels never found our vault to extinguish the flame of
our minds as they did to so many of our brethren."
Mendoça looked at Jamelu again. "I was surprised to
discover this rebel had also been preserved, but
Djamuu will enjoy administering punishment."

All the looted vaults. All the sun eyes knocked from
their pedestals to discharge the energy within and 'kill'
them. Sophie felt sick. She had found her answers
regarding the fate of the Djeen. Civil war had burned
their empire to the ground, but within the vaults,
they'd hidden the seeds of their return. And waited for
someone to wake them.

Mendoça picked through her satchel and
confiscated her lighter, pocketknife, dowsing tools—
anything deemed a threat. Finally he came to her
rumpled stack of origami squares.

"Ah, your hope," he said. The impish smile she'd once admired now mocked her as he tossed the papers over her head like a shower of confetti.

Mendoça gave a nod and the camel drivers finally released her. Blinking back tears of humiliation, Sophie gathered up the scattered papers and clutched them in trembling fists.

"Monster," she said. "I'll never help you find Djamuu."

Mendoça chuckled. "Oh, but you will. Unless you wish to learn about Djeeni torture before you die."

* * *

The dark rock of the Ahaggar Mountains had been worn by wind and weather into curious shapes. Some were broad and domed like turtle shells. Others were steep and slender, resembling twists of smoke or clawing fingers.

Sophie might've enjoyed the display of geologic origami, were it not for the dread in her chest. Mendoça still smiled, still spoke politely, but she knew now it was only the act of an ancient chameleon. He'd talked his way onto many Djeenologist expeditions into the Sahara, hoping each would lead him to Djamuu's vault. When they'd failed, he'd struck them down in anger. Mendoça and his murderous little band were the Order of Djamuu.

No, not Mendoça. Utheel. She'd never known the real Mendoça.

Sophie pulled her camel to a stop to take another reading with her astrolabe. Could she really find the vault in this maze of canyons and peaks? Should she even try? She and Jamelu were both doomed as soon as Utheel got what he wanted.

. . . No, that wasn't Jamelu anymore, either. Shoht was tied atop a camel near the back of the train, guarded by the camel drivers while Utheel kept an eye on her, her revolver tucked in his belt.

Sophie didn't know if Shoht would help her or not, but he was the closest thing she had to an ally now. She'd hoped they might find an opportunity to escape, so she played along, slowing progress as much as she dared, feigning fatigue or the need for extra calculations. This bought her the occasional hour to fold her crumpled papers and contemplate a way out of this nightmare.

But she saw none. Their captors watched them too closely during the day, and at night they were tied to the nearest boulder. Even if they did escape, they wouldn't get far without camels, and those were impossible to steal without notice.

'Do not help them,' Shoht wrote in the dirt one evening as they sat tethered.

'They'll kill us if I don't,' she replied. Their conversations were slow and laborious, each words clumsily drawn with a boot heel. It sometimes took minutes to write a single sentence.

'We are dead already. Djamuu is death.'

'He was evil?' she asked.

'Not always. Each fold corrupts the mind fire, like grains of sand beaten into forged metal. Djamuu became unpredictable, murderous. He slaughtered my village for nothing. I swore to end him and his immortals. We destroyed every sun eye we found, but Djamuu was not among them.'

Sophie frowned. *'If your rebels ended the practice of folding, why were you preserved?'*

'Some thought I would be needed for another rebellion. It should not have been done, but old ways are hard to change. Why did you open the vaults?'

Sophie looked away. *'Your priests were clever. They left instructions on a stone tablet and we followed them. We didn't know the danger.'*

'You were tricked?'

She nodded—a gesture Shoht had learned the meaning of. Unlike her, he was a quick study at languages and had already picked up bits and pieces of English. He also produced the occasional French word, as if Jamelu was still in there somewhere.

Sophie bit her lip. *'Can minds be unfolded?'*

Shoht studied her question in the sand, then shook his head sadly. *'The one before me is only grains of sand now.'* After a pause, he added. *'Soon you will be, too.'*

* * *

The dowsing beads around Sophie's neck crackled with painful energy as they entered a canyon with steep walls of fractured black stone. They were several miles south of where she'd calculated the vault to be, but within the margin of error.

She'd done it. She'd actually found the Vault of Djamuu before any of her academic peers. But the joy she'd once imagined feeling was swallowed by dread. It was too soon. She had no escape plan yet, but it was impossible to hide the discomfort on her face from

Utheel's watchful gaze, nor the snapping sound of the beads.

Grinning, Utheel shouted for their caravan to stop. He dismounted, and using the gauntlets and amber dowsing rods he'd stolen from her, wandered up the canyon in search of the vault's exact location. Sophie and Shoht were dragged off their camels to await his return.

"Now, we *morte*," Shoht muttered to her in stilted English. He glared at their guards who stood a little ways off sipping from a water skin. Shoht looked eager to attack them, but even if his wrists hadn't been bound, his lanky teenage body offered little threat to three grown men.

Sophie's restraints had been removed so she could use the astrolabe while riding, and because she'd convinced Utheel that letting her fingers play with her origami squares steadied her nerves and sped up the search.

When the camel drivers weren't looking, she slipped out the little chip of obsidian she'd scooped from the sandy bottom of a *wadi* during one of their stops. Barely larger than her fingernail, she didn't know if the obsidian flake had been washed there, or dropped by some prehistoric traveler, but it was sharp-edged, and small enough to go unnoticed in her brassiere whenever their captors searched them.

Sophie bent as if to fix her boot laces and pretended to lose her balance. She leaned against Shoht and pressed the obsidian chip into one of his bound hands.

"To escape," she whispered.

Shoht's fingers closed around it with a nod. Sophie then took out her wrinkled squares and continued working on the thick paper glove she'd been weaving from them. It looked more like a badly-knitted oven mitt than a dowsing gauntlet, but paper didn't conduct electricity, and it was the only defense she had.

She tucked the glove back in her pocket when she saw Utheel returning. Judging by the grin on his face, he'd found the keyhole. He led the way back up the canyon, with the camel drivers pushing their prisoners along, to a cleft in the canyon wall. There, he took out her gyroplant.

"Your modern world is a chaotic mess, always on the brink of war," he said, "but I must compliment your machines. This small generator is so much nicer than the sand-driven ones we had."

He spun up the gyroplant and, for the second time in her life, Sophie watched a portal open and stabilize. Even from a several meters away, she could tell the space beyond was massive.

Utheel raised his arms in triumph. "Come! Behold the glory of a real Djeeni vault." He disappeared through the portal and the guards pushed her and Shoht in after him.

Sophie gasped at the riches contained within. Every inch of the domed room's walls were lined with ornate pottery, gilded weapons, richly-carved furniture and colorful jewels.

"Beautiful, isn't it?" Utheel said as he strolled down the central aisle toward the altar. 'Beautiful' was too small a word for the treasures displayed before Sophie, each one a glimpse into the past, into the art and culture of a lost civilization.

It was everything she'd ever hoped to discover, and now she wished she'd never found it.

"Soon, the world will bow to our greatness again," Utheel said, moving further in. One of the guards guided her along after him, while the other two remained near the portal watching Shoht.

"How can Djamuu possibly restore your empire in this modern age?" Sophie asked, growing more worried with each step. "He's only one man."

Utheel turned sharply. "Djamuu is no mere man. Nothing is beyond is abilities! His reign will return stability to this broken world."

Sophie chuckled. "Right. Because your empire was so permanent the first time."

Anger lit Utheel's eyes. "Only because Djamuu was too lenient with his enemies. That mistake will not be repeated. All will praise, or perish!"

Sophie dared not say more. Shoht was right; Utheel's mind was warped from transferring over and over. Or perhaps he and his master had always been as detached from reality as the vaults they'd created.

The stone altar in the center of the room was bigger than most—it needed to be to accommodate the massive sun eye displayed upon it. The size of a bowling ball, the stone's insides were black with folds, as if a storm raged within. The massive stone sphere sat atop a thick glass pedestal, which in turn sat atop a glass tray for additional protection against accidental electric discharge. Clearly they didn't want to lose the 'mind fire' of their precious ruler.

Chanting in Djeeni, Utheel bowed before the altar. He filled a small bowl with gold flakes and stirred in some oil to make a paint. He dipped his thumb in it and turned to Sophie.

She knew what it was. She'd seen pictures of the royal anointing ritual depicted in a dozen different vaults, for a dozen different versions of Djamuu. Sophie blinked in surprise.

"You'd put your precious ruler in a female body?"

Utheel smeared the oil on her forehead with a smirk. "You of any should understand. It is the quality of the brain, not the shape of the body, which matters. Yours is strong and bright, unlike so many in this dark age. You should be honored."

Sophie glanced in Shoht's direction. His face was fixed with concentration, no doubt sawing away at the ropes binding his wrists, cutting one strand at a time with his tiny obsidian blade. There was no way to know how close he was to success. She couldn't count on his help.

There had to be another way out of this mess, because no way was she going to be the latest vessel for some ancient tyrant. But how? No matter how she struggled, she couldn't break her wrists free from the priest holding them. She had to stall.

"A question!" she blurted. "I've earned that much for getting you here."

Utheel sighed, but nodded. "What is it?"

"These vaults. How were they created?"

Utheel chuckled. "A scientist to the end." He set down the bowl. "Come."

He walked to a large gilded chest among the scattered treasures and opened it. The priest holding Sophie shoved her to her knees in front of it.

Inside the chest were ordinary grey rocks. Well, not quite ordinary. She was no geologist, but they looked like fragments of a meteor, and possessed a slight iridescence.

"May I?" she asked. When Utheel nodded, one of her arms was released and she scooped up some of the pebble-sized fragments. They were shockingly heavy, probably about fifteen pounds combined, but otherwise seemed very un-magical.

Utheel must've read the skepticism on her face, for he produced one of her dowsing rods and charged it with the rabbit fur. He then touched it to one of the larger fragments in the chest. The rock made a sound like the striking of a bell and its surface rippled as if made of liquid. The ripples spread, distorting the air around it like a mirage.

"Watch." He plucked a jewel from the nearby piles of wealth, and dropped it above the resonating stone. The jewel plummeted until it reached the distortion waves and then froze in midair. Its descent slowed to a crawl and Sophie watched it fall in slow motion, gradually speeding up as the resonance in the stone faded.

"This gift from the heavens is what Djamuu used to create the vaults. The sun eyes. Everything."

Sophie had never seen anything like it. An unknown element that could manipulate time, or possibly even gravity, to create microcosms. No wonder they hadn't been able to solve the math behind the vaults. These stones made their own little universes where the laws of physics were different.

"Your question is answered," said Utheel, and the priest guarding her grabbed her arm again, shaking it to make her drop the pebbles. Most fell from her grip, but she managed to keep hold of one and slip it into her pocket as she was dragged back to the altar.

Utheel donned her insulated gauntlets and lifted the heavy sun eye from its pedestal. His eyes gleamed with joy as he carried it toward her. "After so many centuries, our god returns!"

Sophie squirmed in her captor's grip. One touch of that giant sphere to her skin and it would be over, but she couldn't break free to reach her own makeshift glove.

Fear swirled through her and once again she was that helpless child crying in the attic, while her uncle stood watching.

"There's nothing wrong with tears, my dear," he would say, "but neither do they change one's circumstances. For that, you must put the head to work."

But she'd *tried* to use her head. Every option was out of reach and she felt like she was bashing her head against a wal—"

Oh. Maybe she could *literally* use her head?

A high-pitched battle cry startled her. Shoht had gotten his hands free and now kicked and rolled as he wrestled with his guards. The ruckus even drew Utheel's attention; he looked away.

Her chance had come.

Sophie threw her head back as hard as she could into the face of the priest behind her. She felt his nose pop as their skulls collided and her own vision filled with flickering stars. The priest howled in pain and his grip relaxed enough for Sophie to jerk her wrists free. She thrust a hand into her pocket and brought it out wearing the thick paper glove.

Utheel turned back, but his reaction was too slow to avoid Sophie's swing. Her gloved hand slapped the sun eye out of his cradling grip. It hit the ground with a thunderous flash of light. The electric charge within it —the ancient mind fire of Djamuu—dissipated harmlessly into the earth. The sphere rolled a little ways before stopping, clear as glass. Djamuu the Eternal was dead.

An anguished, guttural cry broke from Utheel's lips. Face contorted by rage, he reached for Sophie, but the thick gauntlets he wore weakened his grip. She slipped away and raced toward the portal where Shoht still wrestled with the two priests trying to pin him down.

Dropping her shoulder, Sophie slammed into the nearest priest, knocking him into the wealth of furniture and trinkets along the wall. The second priest grabbed her, then screamed when Shoht sank his teeth into the man's arm. Together, they shoved him aside long enough for Shoht to get to his feet.

The priests recovered and their strong hands clawed after them, until a bullet ricocheted off the wall beside Sophie's head. Utheel waved her revolver and charged, screaming incomprehensibly. His compatriots ducked away from the targets of his wrath as he fired wildly.

"Go!" Shoht pushed her up the stairs as more bullets followed. One grazed Sophie's thigh like the touch of hot iron, but she didn't slow until she was through the portal.

Shoht was right behind her and dove into the gyroplant. Orange sparks flew as the device slid out of position and the portal destabilized. Like air rushing back into a vacuum, the portal's distorted edges raced together. The vault closed, cutting off Utheel's angry howl.

Sophie's leg burned, but it was only a scratch. Shoht lay in the sand on his back, panting. A smile spread on his lips for the first time Sophie could remember.

"War is won," he said. And coughed up blood.

Sophie scrambled over to him. More blood stained his chest.

"No," she breathed and pressed her paper glove into the wound to staunch the bleeding. "You can't die on me."

Shoht tried to laugh, but only coughed some more. "Died before you born." He looked at her. "Time slow inside. Utheel dangerous many years yet. Stop others from opening, yes?"

Sophie nodded and lifted a bloodied hand to wipe her nose. Her parents, Uncle Andrew, Jamelu, and now Shoht. Her anger kindled at the thought of standing over yet another grave. Why did it always end like this? It wasn't fair.

Sophie searched her pockets for more paper to staunch the wound and found the meteor pebble. The pebble which slowed time. She squeezed it in her palm. Maybe, just maybe.

Jaw set, Sophie refused to give up.

The Hartford Times, November 1932

Murder in the Sahara!

After another tragic expedition into the Sahara desert, authorities in French Algiers have temporarily suspended all travel by foreign researchers and tourists into the country's interior. The decision comes after young Djeenologist, Sophia Lancaster, and her party were set upon by a merciless pack of bandits. These villains murdered her four compatriots, and briefly took her captive before she managed to escape.

Miss Lancaster claims there were at least fifty of the brigands, and that their leader boasted of sending many explorers to their doom.

Soldiers have been dispatched to hunt down these criminals, but it is uncertain how long it will take to find and neutralize this threat in the vastness that is the Sahara.

EPILOGUE

A cool breeze off the Mediterranean chilled Sophie's skin as she watched the sun set through the window. Her two-story apartment in Oran was small, with earthen walls cracked and stained by age, and a kitchen that was barely more than a fire pit. It was plenty of space for a girl who used to play in an attic.

She hadn't yet wished to return to England and face the Society's ridicule, so when Jamelu's grandfather had offered use of the lodgings, she'd gratefully accepted. And like her attic so long ago, it was a good place to sit and think.

She'd found the answers she sought . . . answers which proved too dangerous to pursue further, or even share with the world. What would she do now? The path she'd followed most of her life had melted away like a mirage. Even the origami square she toyed with refused to take on a satisfying shape. Everything was too familiar. Too stale.

With a sigh, she set the unshaped paper on the desk beside her. With time, a new shape would come. She just needed patience.

Light footsteps crept up the stairs and Sophie turned from the window as Shoht appeared in the open doorway. His arm was still cradled in a sling to keep it still while the muscles in his chest healed, but he was back on his feet now, even if the stairs left him a little out of breath.

It hadn't been easy keeping the gyroplant running while traveling. She'd used her tent to make a stretcher to drag both it and Shoht behind one of the camels, but even that had proved too bumpy and she'd been forced to walk beside it, cranking the handle whenever a fresh jolt made the spinning gears begin to slow.

The effort had been enough to maintain a small bubble of nearly-stopped time around Shoht, until she found a surgeon to stop the bleeding. Five grueling weeks back across the desert had been little more than five minutes for Shoht. She was almost envious. But no, she wouldn't give up that experience. It had taught her just how much she was capable of when she didn't give up hope.

"*Asalaam ealaykum*," Shoht greeted.

Sophie chuckled. "I am the *wrong* person to practice Arabic with."

He returned her smile. When they'd returned to Oran and Shoht could neither speak Berber with Jamelu's family or recall their history together, doctors had conveniently diagnosed him with amnesia. He was learning everything anew.

"How are you getting along as Jamelu?" she asked.

"His family is kind and patient," he answered, moving to the window to share her view of the sunset. "I think they will help."

Shoht had explained his plan to return to the Ahaggar and deal with Utheel and the others once and for all, before any more Djeenologists fell victim to their violence.

"Once Utheel is gone and the stones are cast into the deepest sea," he added, "the vault will be safe for your scientists to find."

"Get rid of the treasure, too," she said.

Shoht frowned in surprise. "You are certain? I would leave it for you."

"That much wealth would only encourage more explorers. No, I only wish to prove my uncle's theory about the currents was correct. When I lead them to the Vault of Djamuu, I want it to be just another barren disappointment like all the others. Perhaps then, interest in the vaults will fade."

Sophie looked down at the miraculous pebble on her desk, so small and plain. The scholar within her ached at the thought of never revealing such a wonder, but the risk of new tyrants rising up to claim its power was too great.

Shoht squinted into the sun. "A heart without greed is rare. Your uncle would be proud."

Sophie smiled at the thought. "I only wish he were alive to share the discovery with."

Shoht nodded solemnly. "The dead live on in our hearts," he said, fingers playing with the edge of his sling. "Tell me about him. It is good to practice my English."

Sophie turned to him. "All right, but only if you tell me about your family, so that they may live on, too."

Appreciation warmed Shoht's smile. "That will take some time."

Sophie watched the red sun hang weightless above the horizon. "Time is something I've got plenty of."

———

As a child, Elin Korund wished her life was as exciting as all the scifi and fantasy movies she watched. These days, she settles for traveling and writing fiction to get her adventure fix. Her story *Quick Cash in the Old Kingdom* appeared in volume 7 of *Unidentified Funny Objects*. When she isn't writing, Elin dabbles in photography, baking, and keeps a sad-looking collection of potted plants.

Down the Rabbit Hole

Susan Conner

The thing about rabbit holes is this: they're *not* just in Alice's Wonderland. They're real, and they're dark and scary. And sometimes you have to go down one. Especially if you've been ordered by your 13-year-old sister, who's three years older and twice your size, to rescue the baby bunnies your pet rabbit Misti gave birth to earlier that day.

It doesn't matter that it's eleven o'clock at night and raining so hard your backyard's a raging river, and you can no longer hear the grinding music and drunken laughter from Mom's party. You agree to ruin your favorite camouflage rain boots by letting them fill up with mud as you stand in the sunken earth hollow that used to be Misti's home. You stick your arm into the opening, feeling past the shivery wet taproots to grab the first two bunnies and hand them to your sister. You have to splat onto your stomach to reach in even further, forever staining your white nightshirt that says *Blondes Have More Fun*. Covered in mud, you grab numbers three and four. You do it because you love Misti way more than you do your boots and your clothes, and, more importantly, you do whatever your sister tells you to do.

But when your sister demands you keep looking, and you have to insert the whole top of your body into a cold, dark tunnel dug by clawed feet, with no air or light or anything to protect you from the squelching mud caving in around you, you might have second thoughts about just how far you're willing to go. Especially when you can't find anything else except earthworms.

I wiggle out of the hole, gasping and bunnyless.

"There aren't any more, Alex," I sputter, swiping mucky strands of hair from my face.

A flash of lightning bisects the night sky, illuminating my sister in her purple hooded raincoat. Towering in majestic monsoon maternity with four bunnies cradled in her arms, she commands: "Look again, Cassie."

And so I crawl back into the rabbit hole, resentful and hopeless. There are no more bunnies down here - why do I always listen to her? But I reach and reach and all of a sudden, I sense it: an unmistakable warmth just inches from my fingertips. I slide in further. I almost pull my arm out of its socket, reaching. I hold my breath, like that's going to help, and maybe it does, because my fingers clamp around a tiny, warm ball of fur.

I squeeze out of the hole, holding a bunny by the wet scruff.

"I got it!"

Cupping it to my muddy nightshirt, I blink away raindrops to look at it shivering against my belly. It's a muddy mess, but it's throbbing, breathing, and its tiny black eyes glisten up at me as if to say *thank you.* I realize this bunny is precious. Without me, it might have died down there in that suffocating hole.

And for that reason, I do not give this last bunny to my sister, no matter how many times she demands. I hold it tight as I trail after her into the house. I don't know if it's a boy or a girl, but I know I'm the one who's going to name it. This mysterious, soggy creature I've just rescued is mine.

*   *   *

After we towel off in the dimly-lit mudroom, Alex pulls a ratty pink Easter basket from the top shelf over the washing machine. She arranges two black and white bunnies on one side, and two gray and white bunnies on the other.

The one I'm holding is solid gray. I crouch and show it to Misti, who's kicking her hind feet against the bars of the cage we temporarily put her in. She calms down, and her nose twitches like she smells something familiar. Alex joins me, unlatching the hutch and setting the basket containing the other four next to her. Misti hops over to them, pushing each one with her nose and darting her pink tongue along their wet, spiky fur.

"Aw, look," Alex says, elbowing me. "A *good* mom."

The door to the kitchen swings open, releasing a stench of smoke and beer, and a confusing barrage of electric guitars and overlapping voices and laughter.

"Did you ssssave the babiesss?" Mom slurs. She steps into the mudroom and peers inside the cage, lifting her pointer finger from her beer bottle to count.

The hairy, bearded man from down the street leans against the open doorway and stares at my mom's butt as she bends over the cage.

"Four bunnies," she moans. Straightening, she takes a woozy step, spotting the little gray bundle in my arms. "Five?"

"High five," drawls the man in the doorway.

Mom puts a hand to her forehead. "What the hell am I gonna do with five bunnies?"

"It's a five-alarm situation." The man snorts, wet and gruff.

"And you, girlie . . ." Mom recoils, wrinkling her nose at me. "You're not coming in the house like that, tracking mud all over my floors."

I pull down awkwardly on the bottom of my slick nightshirt.

"Bath time for baby?" says the man in a soft voice that somehow makes me feel ickier than the mud. A flash of lightning through the window carves hollows in his eye sockets, giving him a skull-face. Shadows from the coatrack add a set of antlers over his scruffy hair.

"I'll make sure she's clean before we come in," Alex replies calmly. Scooping one of the black and white bunnies into her hand, she turns to me and lifts it so its quivering nose takes the place of one of her eyes. She chatters her teeth like she's chomping on a carrot. I laugh.

Mom tosses back the dregs of her beer. "Five bunnies. Couldn't you have left one or two down in the hole?"

"*Mom!*" Alex and I yell at the same time.

"I'm kidding, I'm kidding."

The bearded antler man lumbers up and takes Mom's empty bottle. Squinting down at the bunnies, he drapes an arm around Mom's neck. "I know a guy who can take 'em off your hands."

"Does he mean us or the bunnies?" I whisper to Alex.

"We don't need any help with our pets," Alex says, giving the man one of her meanest, most hate-filled glares.

"Gonna boil them yourself?" he asks, winking at Mom. He leans closer and murmurs loud enough for us to hear, "They make good eating when they're young and tender like that."

Mom makes her loud, trumpeting laugh like she always does when she drinks and some man says something in her ear.

"Oh, come on, Wayne." She gives him a play-slap on the arm. "Let's get back inside. You girls clean up and get to bed. Leave those bunnies in the mudroom. *All* of them," she says with a pointed look at the gray one in my arms.

Hugging my bunny tighter, I run its paper-thin ear through my fingertips as they disappear into the noisy, smoky kitchen.

Alex stabs her middle finger upward at the door when it closes behind them. "Screw you, *Wayndigo*."

"What did you call him?"

"He's a Wendigo," she says, grinding the word between her teeth. "An evil, cannibalistic monster."

I purse my lips, trying to visualize. "Why is he a cannonball?"

Alex sets the black and white bunny back into the cage. "Not cannonball. Cannibal. A person who eats human flesh. A Wendigo devours people, bunnies, everything. It looks like a giant moose, walking on its hind legs. It has a skull face and antlers on its head."

He *did* look like a Wendigo. My chest tightening, I scritch my fingers down my muddy nightshirt, instinctively reaching into a nonexistent pocket. My inhaler's still by my bed.

Alex assumes a dramatic pose, lifting her hands like claws.

"The Wendigo prowls the night for victims while storms rage and the trees shudder in the darkness," she begins in a storybook voice.

"It prowls?" I wheeze, hating my voice for giving away how scared I am.

"And sometimes, over the noise of the wind and the rain and the smacking of its skeletal jaws, you can hear him howl: *Ow-owoooooooooo—*"

"It howls?!"

"Oh, don't be such a baby." Alex drops her arms. "There's no such thing as Wendigos. I'm just teasing."

I hate it when she does that, but I never tell her to stop because she's the big sister and I'm the little one. I'm not supposed to tell her what to do.

She takes the bunny from my hands. "Thanks for going down in there for them, Cassie. You did great. We'll call this one Little Gray."

Little Gray? What kind of boring name is that? Pressing my lips together, I try to figure out a way to disagree with her without making her mad. "Can't I name that one? You can name all the others."

Laughing, she places the bunny into the hutch and latches it. "I've already named them. Boots, Smoky, Shadow, Domino, and Little Gray."

"But . . ."

Pulling a wrinkled nightgown from the pile of clothes on top of the washing machine, Alex pauses, lifting a brow. She doesn't look upset. Just surprised. "But what?"

No matter how hard I try, I can't do it. I can't stand up to her. Little Gray's not as cute as the other names, but it's not *that* bad. I watch it burrow its nose into Misti's belly. "But . . . are we going to leave the bunnies in here all night by themselves? What if the Wendigo takes them?"

Alex sighs, stills my fidgety fingers, and hands me the lilac nightgown. "Don't worry." Her voice sounds soft and hard at the same time. "I'll make sure nothing happens to them."

* * *

That night, I dream of sliding down a muddy hill with a basket of bunnies on my lap. My sister and mom are waiting at the bottom, jumping up and down, clapping and cheering. But then a moose-man stampedes over them, crushing them under his hooves. His jaws open to swallow me and my bunnies as we slide closer and closer.

I sit up in bed with fingers clenched and no air in my chest. Grabbing my puffer from the nightstand, I inhale and tell myself to relax. It was just a dream. But the bunnies are real! Little Gray and her four siblings. I hop up to use the bathroom before I go check on them.

When I get out, I notice the door to Alex's room is open. Her bed's already made, which is weird because she hates making her bed almost as much as I do.

Picking my way around bottles, over crushed fast-food bags, and past Mom's party friends asleep on the sofa, I open the mudroom door as softly as possible so I won't frighten the bunnies.

They're gone. No basket. No bunnies. Just Misti, who's hop-pacing the cage, kicking the bars with her hind feet as she turns. She pauses to stare at me with her ears pressed back, her glassy eyes wild and frantic.

My heart slamming against my chest, I race back into the house, searching for Alex. I don't want to yell and wake up anyone, because I've done that before and adults with hangovers are not nice and they're not friendly and I wish they'd go home, why are they always over here making such a mess of our place, stinking it up with beer and cigarettes, they need to go home, just go home, and where is Alex??

I try the door to Mom's bedroom. It's locked. Pressing my ear to it, I can hear Mom snoring. I can't imagine Alex would be in there with her. They're always fighting, especially after a party.

Maybe she took the bunnies outside. Running to my room, I grab my inhaler and head to the mudroom again, where I slip on my camo boots. They're wet, muddy, and cold on my bare feet. Between that and my thin lilac nightgown, I'm freezing as I squelch out back. At least it's stopped raining. The sky is blue and the sun is shining brighter than normal. Droplets of water jiggle on the leaves, glistening like twinkle lights. Something purple lies on the ground by the fence, next to Misti's hole.

I hurry over to it as quick as I can without getting my boots stuck in the muck. A small river of rainwater cascades off as I pick it up. Alex's raincoat. Shaking it out, I examine the muddy entrance to Misti's home. It's not collapsed like I thought it was after I wiggled out with Little Gray last night. And it's gotten bigger. A lot bigger. Like, I could sit down and slide right in.

Shivering, I slip on the raincoat and put my inhaler in the pocket. My fingers brush against paper. I pull it out. It's a note, in Alex's handwriting.

Cassie, I took the bunnies.

I flip the note over, but there's nothing on the other side. I study the muddy hole in the ground. Where did she take them? Down there? Why? The only reason I can think my sister would get dirty by crawling into a muddy rabbit hole is if she was being chased. But by who? Or what? Something that prowls. Something that howls. Something like a Wendigo.

I swallow nervously, stuffing the note back into my pocket and leaning down to look inside the hole.

"Alex?" I call.

No response.

It's so dark in there. What if the Wendigo is inside, with his skeleton jaws open, waiting to eat me? What if he's already eaten Alex and the bunnies?

Resisting the urge to take another hit on my puffer, I sit down before I can change my mind. I slip my boots and legs into the opening, then crick my neck until I'm completely inside with my head tilted to the side. A few spidery roots dangling down from the top tickle my cheek, but it's so dark I can't even see them.

Feeling around for the tunnel wall next to me, my hands flap into empty air. Where's the tunnel? I scooch further into the hole until I can straighten my neck. I wait until my eyes adjust to the dark and then I stand up.

No. Way.

I can't believe this. It's impossible. I'm standing fully upright not more than a foot underground, inside a ginormous earth cavern that's at least as high as my bedroom ceiling. The dirt walls surrounding me have deep vertical grooves scraped into them, as if they were dug by giant fingernails. Pale, knobby roots as wide as my body twist down from the top, embedded in the dirt, crisscrossing over one another and spreading every which way like giant cracks. Some of them poke up from the floor, branching into arm- and finger-width tendrils.

The air's so cool down here. Crisp and clean. Earthy and . . . I don't know what it reminds me of, but it's familiar. Something I haven't smelled in a while, but I recognize it, just like how Misti knew the scent of her babies in her hutch last night.

Spreading my arms, I inhale. My lungs open up like they want to hug everything around me. The gunk and phlegm that's been clogging up my chest ever since I was born disappears. Whatever is down here, I'm not scared anymore. I'm excited. This is *my* world, and this is where I belong. It might be an impossible world that goes against everything I know and have ever learned about in school, but in here, I can do anything. Like find my sister and rescue five bunnies.

I breathe in the fresh air again, and I know what it is I'm smelling.

It's the smell of *adventure!*

* * *

Thirteen . . . Fourteen . . . I'm feeling a little less adventurous after this many times circling the cavern, looking for a way down. Except for the entrance, there are no other tunnels. But Alex and the bunnies must have gone somewhere.

"Where did they go?" I cry.

"WhereDidTheyGo-go-go?" echoes back in an overlapping sing-song.

That was pretty cool.

"Echo!" I call.

"Echo-Echo-Echo! Hello?"

I freeze, one boot atop the knot of a root on the ground. "Hello?" My voice comes out faint and whispery, barely audible over the pounding of my heart.

"Helloooooo, little girl with the muddy boots boots boots! Could you please not step step step on us?"

The root underneath my boot sinks into the soil, and suddenly, every root along the floor, ceiling, and walls shifts to the left with a slithery noise.

I swallow, turning a slow circle in the middle of the cavern. "Who's talking?"

"Talking, talking, talking," responds the voice from everywhere at once.

Only, I realize it's not a single voice. It's hundreds of voices, speaking in unison, hitting all the notes on a musical scale, like a family sing-along featuring everything from high-pitched baby voices to deep grandpa voices.

"We are tired of talking," they sing. "And being trampled trampled trampled on. At least the little girl before you was kind kind kind enough to remove her shoes shoes shoes before entering our brand new home home home."

"The little girl before me?" I ask. "Did she have a basket of bunnies? That's my sister! Where'd she go? I need to find her."

"Find her, find her, find her you should. Before she is lost, lost, lost forever. A world like this is no place for little girls girls girls playing tricks on their sisters."

"My sister wasn't playing a trick. She was running away from a Wendigo."

"Wendigo-gito-wendo-what-o?" The voices sound out the word as if they've never heard it before. The smaller taproots sticking up from the ground wave and lean toward one another, murmuring in concerned-sounding echoes.

"It's an evil, cannonball—I mean, cannibal—monster," I tell them. "It wants to eat the bunnies we rescued last night."

"Ah! Was it you you you who stuck your hand down the hole hole hole and created this lovely living room room room?"

I don't know how that's possible. But they sound pleased and maybe they'll help me if I say yes. "That was me. Our pet rabbit Misti had five bunnies that were going to drown if we didn't get them out of the monsoon. I hope I didn't hurt you."

"You cannot hurt us. But why did your sister bring them back back back in a basket? She would not answer when we asked asked asked."

Pulling out my sister's note, I examine it again. *I took the bunnies.* Could she really be playing a trick on me? Trying to scare me, like when she teased me about the Wendigo?

"Can you please tell me where my sister went?" I ask the worms as politely as possible, even though I'm starting to get steamed.

"Down down down."

"Down where?"

"To the party party party."

A party? Now I'm really mad.

"Can you show me the way to this party?"

"Only if you have an invitation-on-on."

I flap Alex's note in the air. "It's right here. It's even addressed to me: Cassie."

"Very well, Cassie-sassy-sassy."

I've been called lots of things, mostly *Baby* by my sister, and *Girlie* by my mom. Never *Sassy*. I like it.

The roots shift in unison again, slinking along the walls with weird sucking noises as they pop in and out of the earth like one long earthworm. They move in a counter-clockwise motion, not fast enough to make me dizzy, but enough to make me wonder if I'm standing or moving.

Tottering a bit to one side, I prop my hand against the clammy wall to steady myself, then pull it back when a root emerges underneath it. "Excuse-use-use us. Do you want to go down the slide, or not-ot-ot?"

A slide? Like, the mudslide in my dream? Maybe I'm still dreaming. But one look at the humming, echoey root worms slithering in and out of the dirt and I know my dreams are not this crazy.

The worms loop over one another as if they're weaving a friendship bracelet. A hole opens up in the floor and down they spiral, forming a curving chute that stretches into the darkness.

"Am I supposed to go down this?" I ask doubtfully.

"You're not supposed to do anything-thing-thing," respond the voices. "Except whatever you want to do-do-do."

Huh. What do I want to do-do-do? Have I ever had to really decide before-for-for? Usually my sister or mom figure it out-out-out for me. Oh my God, I'm thinking in echoes. I've got to get out of here before I lose lose lose it!

Plunking down on the top of the root-worm slide, I brace my hands against the slippery sides.

"You're sure my sister's down here?" I ask, squinting into the void below.

"Here here here," they echo, not really answering my question.

"No, I mean, is this where the party isssssssssss—"

Something pushes my shoulder blades, and I'm off. Flying, careening, sliding down the spiral chute, feeling exactly like I did in the first part of my dream. I should try to stop myself, but I can't because it's so fast.

And slick.

And fun!

"*Whooo-hoooooooo!*" I cry, raising my hands like I'm on a roller coaster.

This ride is way better than anything I've been on at the state fair, and I didn't have to grovel for Mom to pay for my ticket or stand in a long line.

"*Whooo-hoooooooo!*" I cry, raising my hands, my sister's purple raincoat flapping behind me like a super-hero cape.

Neon lights blur by in a dizzy spiral—so cool! And so many. Endless loops of light going around and around and around.

"Whooo-hoooooooo!" I cry, raising my hands like I'm on a tilt-a-whirl, wondering when it's going to end. I'm getting a little nauseous.

"Whoo—" Gulp.

Keep it down, Cassie, keep it down. Don't spew, don't spew, don't—

"Whoo . . ."

Do. NOT. Spew.

Swallowing hard, I lower my arms. If I ever unclench my jaw, I am going to die on this ride, choking on my own vomit.

La, la, la, la, la sing the root-worms underneath me. Have they been singing this whole time? I guess I'd been too busy whooping and hollering to notice. The sound is very soothing. I relax as I continue to descend. I pick a few dried clumps of mud from my hands, thinking about Alex.

If she's in trouble and took the bunnies down here to escape the Wendigo, why did she tell the worms she was looking for a party? On the other hand, if she's really going to a party, why would she take the basket of bunnies? Neither scenario makes sense, but I don't think she'd come down here willingly. This place is too weird for a logical 13-year-old like Alex who's always telling me what to do.

I giggle, wondering what she thought about sliding down a spiral made of singing earthworms? I bet she really freaked. I bet it fried her brain, haha.

Ha ha ha.

Suddenly, I fly off the end of the slide into the darkness. *KERPLOP.* I land feet first in what sounds like a shallow pond.

I flail my arms to get my balance. It's so dark. What happened to the pretty lights? Where am I?

Crazy laughter rollicks overhead.

Hah hahahhaha ahahahaha

      hahah ahahahHAHAhaha Ahaha   ah

Ha

    Hahaha

  Ahahah

 AahahahahahaAHAHA

Oh, no.

I know that laugh.

It's Mom's.

Totally drunk. Like, whenever her party friends are supposed to come by, and she's already downed the first six-pack and Alex gets mad. *Oh, who cares?* Mom laughs. *Ha! Ha ha ha ha! My friends know how hard I work to pay the bills and buy clothes and video games for my children. No thanks to their lame-o baby-daddies. HA! Who supports this fam? Me. I deserve to have a little fun once in a while. HA hahAhaHa . . .*

The laughter fades. The fresh air is gone. It smells like stale beer. I can't hear anything except a slow, eerie, dripping sound. Followed by a hiccup.

"Is that you, Mom?" I whisper nervously.

It was funny to think of Alex in this strange world, but the idea that *Mom* might be here makes my stomach clench. I feel guilty, like I'm the one who created this weirdness, and me, my sister and the bunnies getting lost down here is all my fault.

A blue glow pulsates a few feet away. It's coming from a bottle, sitting atop a rock ledge. Something moves inside the bottle, flickering like a trapped, neon firefly. Next to it, another bottle lights up, only pink. Then, a green one. Yellow, purple, orange . . . different colors come to life inside dozens of bottles perched around the rock walls.

I start toward them, but I can't lift my feet. My boots are sunk deep into the mud.

"Help!" I call, hoping the singing worms might rescue me. But they're gone. The spiral slide has disappeared. I'm alone in the middle of a sinkhole.

"Looks like you're stuck," laughs a voice from somewhere above me.

Squinting into the darkness, I can barely make out two feet dangling down. They look like . . . monkey feet. Toes wiggling, they swing up and over to my left, then to my right in a zig-zag pattern toward a basket sitting on the edge of some rocks. Releasing what must be an invisible vine, a small creature plops down on the rock ledge and turns around.

I've never seen anything like it: not in the zoo, not on TV, not on the Internet. It's a monkey. Only it's not. It has monkey arms and legs, but no tail. It's hairless, with wrinkly orange skin on a flat, round body that looks like a deflated basketball. Leaning an elbow on a boulder, it scratches its long nose, which is in the shape of a trumpet.

"How are you gonna get out of that sinkhole?" it asks and hiccups.

I try lifting my boots. They sink further into the mud.

Reaching out a hand, I do my best to limit the panic in my voice. "Won't you help me?"

*Tsk*ing, the monkey creature plunges its trumpet nose into the mud and makes a loud slurping noise. It sucks and sucks, and the mud around my boots goes down to my heels.

"Thank you," I say, pulling on my feet. But the boots still won't budge.

"Those are cool boots," notes the orange monkey as it wipes the back of its palm across its nose. "I wouldn't mind having a pair of camo rain boots, ahaHaha HA hA ha."

There's that crazy Mom-laugh again.

"How do I get out of this mud?"

"Just step out of your boots."

"But I'll sink!"

"Maybe you will, maybe you won't, haha."

I narrow my eyes. I can't decide if it's serious or teasing. That's when I notice the Easter basket perched on the rocks behind it. A set of bunny ears pokes up from inside and my heart skips a beat.

"Where did you get that basket of bunnies?" I ask, pointing.

"From the girl before you."

"Did you steal them from her?"

"HA HA HA ha HA HA HA! Of course not. It was a trade."

"She traded you the bunnies? For what?"

"Directions to a party."

That doesn't sound like Alex.

The monkey lifts an arm to scratch its armpit. "Shall we, haHaha, make a trade of our own? Say, the basket of bunnies for your boots?"

I look down at my boots stuck in the mud. I love these boots. I don't want to lose them. But there's no question for me. I love Misti's babies more.

"Okay, but you also have to tell me the way to the party."

"Oh, haHAha, you can't have it all, girlie. It's either the bunnies or directions, not both."

"*Ow-owooooooooooooo,*" comes a deep, bloodcurdling howl from far above me.

"What was that?" I gasp, almost falling as I peer into the pitch-black darkness overhead. "That sounded like . . . like the Wendigo."

"A Wendigo?" chatters the monkey gleefully. "They like to eat little girls, haha, almost as much as they like to eat bunnies."

I gulp.

"You'd better hurry and make up your mind, haHAhAhA. Which do you want? Bunnies or party?"

"The bunnies."

"Ha! I'll drink to that." Jumping up to grab onto an invisible vine, the monkey swings victoriously across the sinkhole to the opposite side and grabs a bottle. At first, I think it's going to throw it at me, but it pulls out a cork and gulps down the emerald green glow inside. "Okay, girlie. Gimme yer boots."

"How can I give them to you? You're supposed to get me out, first."

"Hahahah. Nothing in the contract about helping you out of the mudhole. Just step out of the boots. You won't sink, I promise." It tosses the empty bottle into the muddy water. Where it promptly sinks.

The distant howls grow louder. The Wendigo is sliding down after me, and I've got to get out of here before it lands on top of me and eats me. But if I step out of my boots, I'll get sucked into the mudhole. Maybe I can pull myself out on one of those invisible vines.

Squinting into the dark overhead, I reach up, feeling around in the air. My fingertips brush against something wispy, but it's too high for me to grab.

"Oh, hahahAha hA!" laughs the creature. "Easier for the other girl, she was much taller."

Standing on my toes, I take a breath, bend my knees, and jump. I don't get far, because my feet are still stuck inside my boots, but it's enough to latch onto a rough, invisible rope. I pull and pull, popping my feet out of the boots. As I haul myself up, I focus on my breathing to block out the monkey's laughter and the Wendigo's howling. Kicking my legs, I swing to the rock ledge and drop down next to the basket. I grab it and count.

Only four bunnies. Where's Little Gray? Did Alex lose her? Or did she take her to the party with her? My chest tightens as I frantically search around the basket. The bottles nearby brighten as if helping me look.

"These boots are great, haHa ha HAHAhaha!"

The hairless orange monkey already has my boots on its skinny legs. It parades around on the other side of the rock ledge, kicking up water, splashing, and laughing.

"*Ow-owoooooooooooooo!*" This howl sounds even closer.

"How do I get to the party?" I plead.

But the monkey doesn't answer. It's too busy admiring my boots.

I search the rock ledge, hoping to find a gap big enough for me to squeeze through.

"Ouch!" I wince as the sharp rocks poke the bottoms of my feet. I stumble into a bottle, catching it before it topples down the ledge.

"Thank you," says a very proper-sounding voice. From inside the bottle.

I bring it up to examine it. On the other side of the glass, a fluttery moth stares back with clear, bulbous eyes underneath two black antennae. A double set of neon blue wings flaps rapidly on either side of its Q-tip body.

"Let us out, love, and we'll show you the way to the party," it promises, pronouncing the last word 'pahrty'.

Hurriedly, I uncork the bottle, then grab all the bottles around me to do the same. A cloud of twinkling moths surrounds me.

"Hey," barks the monkey, no longer laughing. "Those are mine!"

The moths flutter into a line that winds to the top of the rocks. Gritting my teeth, I scramble over the sharp rocks as fast as I can in bare feet with the basket of bunnies in hand.

The monkey jumps off the rock ledge, making a beeline for us. "Stop!"

But it's the one who stops. Right in the middle of the mudhole, where I got stuck. It looks down at my camo rain boots filling up with mud.

"Nooooo!" it wails.

Turning my back on the sinking monkey, I hurry after the moths. They disappear into a small, tight crevasse that would have been invisible if it hadn't been for their glowing wings. It's so small, the basket won't fit. I put two bunnies in the left pocket of Alex's raincoat, and the other two in the right, then squeeze through sideways. There's no way the Wendigo will be able to fit through here.

When I straighten, I find myself in what appears to be a tall, narrow elevator shaft. The moths light it up like a kaleidoscope as they flutter upward.

Before I can open my mouth to ask where we are, a brisk wind sweeps under my feet. Up I fly.

* * *

Up air shafts, down worm slides, over invisible ropes . . . Strange creatures talking to me, singing, lighting my way . . . it's way more interesting underground than it is up-top. If it weren't for the boot-stealing monkey and the threat of a flesh-eating Wendigo, I think I could get used to this world.

As I soar up in the narrow shaft, I wrap my coat around me tightly, peeking inside the pockets to check the bunnies. The air parts the fur on their little heads, flattening them down like bald baby combovers.

An orange moth darts in front of my nose, making me go cross-eyed. I know a moth can't really be glowing this bright (which it is, brighter than a Halloween glow stick), nor should it have arms to point (which it does, at something over my head and to the left), nor can it speak with a *Great British Bake Off* accent (which it can, telling me to "have a grahnd time," and "mind the brolly," whatever that means). And it's even more impossible for it to insert two fingers into its mouth and give a whistle loud enough to make my ears ring. A dozen or more glowing moths flutter up, hauling a stick. No, it's not a stick. It's a black umbrella with a curved handle.

They hook it over my arm and arrange themselves into an arrow shape, pointing at a spot above my head.

"Your exit's coming up, love," yells the orange moth over the noise of the air rushing by. Using its impossible arms, it mimics opening the umbrella and holding it over its antennaed head.

Clamping one arm around my coat and lifting the umbrella with the other, I press the button and it pops open. My arm jerks in the socket as I come to a complete stop. The rest of the glowing moths zip by me, waving and calling "Cheers!" and "Ta!" Down I float, Mary Poppins-style, to land on a platform jutting out from the side of the shaft. I step away from the edge and clang into a rusty metal ladder, like the kind they put in sewers.

I hesitate, expecting some kind of new creature to magically appear and lift me up by the shoulders.

No?

Guess not.

I start climbing toward the square trap door at the top.

As I get closer, the ladder vibrates under my bare feet from a steady, thumping rhythm, like music is playing nearby. The sound goes from muffled to deafening when I push open the trap door. Whoa. It's the kind of music Alex loves: rappy, gangy, slangy.

Clambering up, I step into a war zone. Or maybe it's tornado alley.

Whatever it is, it's a mess. Like a big, underground garbage bin. Everywhere I look, there are piles and piles of *stuff*: the kinds of things you find when you pull up a sofa cushion. Only, they're fifty times their normal size. Cigarette butts as big as rolling pins, bottle caps bigger than crockpots, crumpled mountains of fast-food wrappers, giant coins, sled-sized barrettes, towering pencils, and, ew, is this Alex's retainer I'm hiding behind?

This junk must be from our house. How did it get here, and why is everything so big?

As the beat dies down between songs, a burst of laughter rises up on the other side of the retainer. I peek around, then dive back under cover.

Rats!

I look again, hoping I'd hallucinated. No. It's a pack of rats. And not just any old rats: they're giant rats the size of greyhounds.

They blend into the litter with their matted gray fur and naked tails. Rooting around in the junk, they lift things to their whiskered noses and sniff. After a couple nibbles, they jabber-snark, laugh, then toss away the leftovers, making even more of a mess. A new song comes on and they roar, making gangster signs with their long claws and tapping their tails to the beat.

I'm so busy watching them, I almost jump out of my skin when I hear a sneeze next to me. Brushing the cold, wet spray from my arm, I come face to face with an oversized rat standing on its hind legs, staring at me with beady black eyes. It wipes its whiskers with the back of a clawed paw.

I have two choices.

One is to scream.

The other is to say, "God bless you."

And hope it's the right choice.

The rat flutters its claws into happy-claps. "How surprising to meet such a polite human. Thank you."

"You're welcome," I say in relief. But I put my hands in my pockets over the bunnies to be on the safe side.

"Did you just arrive?" the rat wheezes in a friendly man's voice. "Can I get you something? A crumb of moldy cheese to nibble on? A nice, hard ball of chewed gum? I hear there's some tasty dregs of beer left in that bottle if you crawl inside."

"No, thank you. I'm looking for my sister. Have you seen her?"

"Well, what does she look like?"

"Like me, only taller, and more . . . filled out. And she has dark, curly hair instead of straight blonde. And her skin's darker than mine." Actually, I hadn't really thought much about it before, but now that I'm describing Alex, it occurs to me how totally different we are. She doesn't have the same dad as me, but I'm so used to looking at her and thinking she's me because we do almost everything together and whatever she thinks and says is what I think and say. It's weird to suddenly realize she's her and I'm me.

"Oh yes. A tall, dark-haired girl came earlier. I believe she went—" The rat pauses to suck in a raspy-sounding breath, slapping a claw to its chest. "Sorry," it squeaks in a pinched-off voice. "Asthma."

I know that feeling. I've had it my whole life.

I pull my inhaler from my pocket. "Here, try this."

The rat waves its hands, its cheeks turning blue as it gasps, "No, no, I'm on the wagon."

"Is that what this is?" I ask, looking around the mess. It doesn't look like a wagon to me. More like . . . the crawl space underneath our house.

Lifting its nose in the air as if hunting molecules, the rat shakes its head. "I'm not drinking or smoking anymore. Not even e-cigarettes."

"Oh, okay. But this is Albuterol. It helps you breathe. Press down here while you inhale."

The rat takes it from me with a skeptical-but-hopeful grimace and breathes in a puff.

Blinking in time to the music, a smile stretches its mouth as it takes a deep, wheeze-free inhale, then another, and another. It looks at the inhaler clutched in its claws. "Oh my goodness. Where did you find this?"

"I didn't find it. Mom bought it at the pharmacy."

"Well, some day you must show me where this farm is located." The rat offers the inhaler back to me, but I shake my head.

"You keep it," I tell him. "I don't need it anymore. But what I *do* need is to find my sister. Can you tell me where she is?"

"Yes, yes. Follow me!"

Winding our way through the trash, I step carefully over giant rubber bands, around a set of shrub-sized car keys, and past a line of transparent yellow pillars that I realize are empty prescription drug bottles. We make a left at an SUV-sized sandal that is so moldy and stinky, my eyes water. Going down a carpet of greasy receipts, I trip over a set of tweezers so long and rusty, they could be fireplace tongs. We finally reach a round hut made of log-sized pellets that look like Misti's rabbit food. A Queen of Hearts playing card serves as a door. The rat pushes it open and peers inside. Turning, he puts a claw to his lips. "She's asleep."

Asleep?

I brush aside the playing card and walk in. A figure in familiar blue pajamas is curled up on the floor.

"Alex!" I yell. "How can you be sleeping?"

"Is that you, Cassie?" Sitting up slowly, Alex sniffles and wipes away tears.

I can't believe it. Alex is crying. I've never *ever* seen her cry. Now I feel bad for yelling at her. Hurrying over, I drop to my knees and put my arms around her. "It's me. I'm here."

"Cassie, Cassie . . ." Alex sobs into my hair. Raising her head, she looks around the hut, then latches onto my shoulders with frantic eyes. "I'm still dreaming!"

"No, you're awake," I tell her, slipping out of her grip.

"No, no. I'm asleep. My old iPhone playlist keeps repeating over and over. Do something to wake me up, Cassie. Slap me, hit me, punch me!"

Tempting, but: "I'm not going to hit you, Alex."

I pluck a black and white bunny from my pocket and brush its soft fur against her cheek instead. "See? You're awake. I found the bunnies. Well, all of them except for—"

"Little Gray! I hid her in my pocket." Alex checks her pajamas, pats the ground around her, then jumps up and circles the hut. "Where did she go?"

"You lost her?"

Kneeling next to me, Alex takes the black and white bunny and presses it to her chest, muttering fast and low as though she's talking more to herself than me. "No, I couldn't have lost her. None of this is real. It's just a dream. I fell asleep in the mudroom. I dreamt a Wendigo came in. I ran outside with the basket of bunnies and heard Mom laughing from Misti's rabbit hole. *Come to the party,* she said. *You'll be safe down here!* I started to write you a note. But then I heard the Wendigo howl so I dove down the hole. There were these giant talking worms that pushed me down a slide, and Mom turned into a nasty orange monkey who tricked me into giving up the basket. I floated up to another place with rats as big as dogs and giant pieces of trash all over—"

"Did you see your gargantuan retainer?" I can't keep myself from interrupting with a giggle. "So gross!"

Alex freezes, her mouth in an O shape. Her hands are clenched so tight around the bunny, I fear it'll get crushed. I gently lift her fingers and put it back into my pocket.

"What happened to Little Gray?" I prompt, since Alex still hasn't snapped out of it.

"I don't know." She says each word slowly, like she does when Mom asks where her report card is. "But if you're seeing the things I'm dreaming about, it must mean you're not real, either. You're just part of my dream."

At this, I *do* slap her. Not hard. Just a swat on the arm.

Alex jumps, looks down at her arm, then back up at me.

"I'm not asleep."

"Nope."

She swallows, looking around. "Then what the hell is going on, Cassie? What is this place?"

I follow her gaze. "I think it's a hut made of giant rabbit pellets."

"But, *where* are we?" Now she's sounding more like my sister: impatient.

"Underground."

"That's not possible."

"Why not? It's like Alice in Wonderland."

"That's a story, Cassie. Someone wrote it. It's not reality. Do you think . . . do you think we've been drugged? Kidnapped? Maybe we're dead . . ."

Her attitude is pissing me off. She's forgotten how to have an adventure. "You're always trying to explain everything all the time. Did you hear the worms singing when you were on the slide? Wasn't it fun?"

"*Fun?*" She shakes her head at me. "How are you not freaked out by any of this?"

I think back to what Mom said to Alex when she went to the pet store last month to get us a puppy, and came home with Misti instead. "I prefer the unusual," I say.

"Tell me something I don't know," Alex mutters. She runs her fingers through her black curls and takes a deep breath, which I think means she's going to stop arguing with me.

"Let's go find Little Gray," I suggest, hopping to my feet. "Maybe my rat friend saw her. I'll ask."

But before I can reach the door, the playing card swings open and in rushes the rat with my puffer raised to its snout. It takes a deep inhale, then lowers the Albuterol and says in a pinched voice, "We have a party-crasher."

"Is it a little gray bunny?" I ask hopefully.

"No, it's a . . . erm, I don't know what it is, but it's *definitely* not polite."

"*Ow-owooooooooooo!*"

"The Wendigo!" I gasp. How did it get up here? There's no way it could've fit through that tiny crack.

Alex is right beside me, sinking her fingernails into my arm.

We tip-toe to the door and push it aside to peek out. Over the twisted, tangled mess of junk, a tall figure is moving, swinging his antlers to and fro as he nears the prescription pill bottles.

"Is there another way out?" Alex whispers to the rat.

"Yes, I'll show you!" The rat scampers out the door.

Alex and I start after it, but as soon as we're outside the hut, I latch onto the back of her PJ's, halting her.

"What about Little Gray? We can't leave without her."

Alex's face assumes the Big Sister look. Tight lips. Scowly brows. "There's no time to look for her. We have to get out of here before I lose my mind!"

"I can't believe you. You're the one who made me crawl back down the hole for Little Gray, and now you want to abandon her?"

"We are leaving, Cassie. NOW." Alex grabs my arm. I shake her loose.

"No."

Alex blinks in shock. I thought *I* was surprised at how forceful that word came out, but she's totally blown away. Lips parted. Brows up.

"Cassie, be real. You can't find a tiny bunny in this huge mess," she sputters.

"Don't tell me what I can and can't do." I square my shoulders. This must be how superheroes feel. Confident. Sure.

Suddenly, I'm picturing how different our relationship is going to be if we get out of here alive. No more caving in to every little order Alex gives me. I'll stand up for myself. We'll fight and argue and things between us will be loud and challenging and way more fun than they've ever been. The love I feel for myself, my sister, and all our future disagreements swells my heart just like the Grinch's when the Whos sing their Christmas song. I am fired up. I am ready to find this bunny, go back home, and borrow all the clothes I've ever wanted to take out of Alex's closet but was too scared to ask.

A swooshing sound sails over our heads. We duck as a giant, number 2 pencil pierces the hut behind us, collapsing the roof and spilling pellets at our feet.

Slipping off the purple raincoat, I check to make sure all four bunnies are in the pockets before handing it to Alex. "Keep them safe. I'll find Little Gray and meet you outside."

I'm off before she can say anything, hopping over pellets, moving aside clothespins, looking underneath gum wrappers, crouching low so the Wendigo won't see me. I peer into giant straws and search a suitcase-sized coin purse. Nothing.

"Ow-owooooooooooo!"

The howling is so close! But I don't dare straighten to find out how close. Something catches my eye underneath the stinky sandal. I race toward it and do a belly-flop, just like I did to reach into Misty's hole. Holding my breath from the stench, I feel around the sticky floor with my hand. Sure enough, I sense it again: warmth just out of reach of my fingertips. I reach and reach, hoping it's not a Wendigo foot. I shove my arm as far as it will go. My hand locks around a ball of fur.

Little Gray!

"Cassie, watch out!" Alex cries from far away.

I look up. Above me towers the Wendigo. Two hollowed-out eye sockets stare down at me. They're big and black and set deep in his skull. Sharp, jagged teeth are bared in an evil smile. Saliva drips down in a long, gooey string, stretching to the floor and pooling next to my elbow. I don't move. I don't even breathe.

Raising one skeletal arm, the Wendigo makes a grab for me. With a cry, I tuck Little Gray to my chest and roll to the side, looking up just in time to see a log-shaped pellet fly overhead. It clips the Wendigo's antlers. He stumbles backward and crashes into the pill bottles. They topple over him like dominoes.

"Come on, Cassie, let's go!" yells my sister.

I don't mind obeying this order. I jump up and race toward her, my bare feet slipping and sliding on the greasy receipt, which, in a situation that didn't involve running away from a Wendigo, I would have called fun. I clamber up an old phone book where Alex and the rat are standing next to a glowing white rectangle that looks like the iPhone she lost last fall. Alex has a stash of rabbit pellets in her arms, and the rat wields the tong-sized tweezers, a rubber band attached to the pointed ends.

"We made a slingshot!" Alex announces, dumping her armful of rabbit food at my feet. Her brown eyes are lit up every bit as bright as those moths that led me here.

"That was awesome," I pant, grinning. I haven't seen her this happy in eons. She's smiling wide enough for me to see her teeth! "It was a great shot."

The rat points at the USB charging cord running from the iPhone to a triangle of light in the wall. "Follow the singing creature's tail. It will lead you out."

"Thank you," I tell him sincerely. Before I can think too much about it, I plant a kiss on his whiskered cheek. "Goodbye."

I didn't know rats could blush, but I guess if they can use inhalers, their cheeks can turn pink, and that's what his do.

Alex takes my hand. Together we climb over combs and clips, soggy newspapers and crumpled tin foil, following the cord to the patch of light. As we get closer, I spy thick, green blades of grass as tall as trees on the other side. My belly flutters in nervousness: is everything going to be just as big out there?

Dropping my hand, Alex slips through the crack and the light vanishes like something's blocking it.

"Oh my God, such a rush!" Alex's voice booms. I'd swear it's coming from a speaker in the sky, it's so loud.

A giant brown eyeball peeks through the crack. Thick, dark lashes as long as bird feathers fan a breeze on my face.

"Cassie? We were underneath the foundation of our house. I don't know how, but once you come out, you'll be back to normal!"

I pull Little Gray to eye level. "Are you ready?"

I kiss her nose, then scooch her through the crack. It fills with fluffy gray fur until fingers clamp around the bunny and lift her out of the way.

"I've got her," confirms my sister. "Your turn."

I take one last inhale of the cool, underground air. It's not as fresh as when I first came down the rabbit hole. In fact, it reeks of garbage and moldy things, but, in a way, it still smells like *adventure*.

I step through the crack.

Only I don't step through it. I explode. At least, that's what it feels like. My head sails off my neck and —*whee!*—soars straight up into the blue sky while the rest of me splinters in different directions. My left arm goes one way, my right arm goes another, my right leg flies in front of me, and my left falls behind, and it doesn't hurt—it tingles. I don't know how long it lasts. It feels like forever and it feels like just a second before all my body parts come back together like a reverse Humpty-Dumpty and—*bam!*—I fall to the ground on my belly.

That *was* a rush!

I roll over as Alex races up to me. I hold out my hands, thinking she's going to help me up, but instead, she slips her arms underneath my armpits and pulls. I feel like I'm being torn in pieces again, only this time it hurts.

"Let go of her, you monster!" Alex screams.

That's when I realize part of me is trapped. A skeletal arm protrudes from the crack in the foundation, its fingers clamped around my left ankle. I kick as Alex pulls, but the hand won't let go. If anything, it tightens. As Alex inches me away from the crack, the arm stretches, growing fleshier and more human. Alex gives a mighty heave like she's going to tear me in two. My ankle slips free and out flies a body, nearly crushing us as we tumble to the side.

It's Wayne. Wayndigo!

Moaning, he rolls onto his stomach. Blood trickles from the top of his forehead where his thick, scruffy hair dips back. Woozily raising his head, he glares at me and Alex, saliva drooling from the corner of his bearded lips. Alex's arms tighten around me. I can feel her shaking just as much as I am.

Little Gray hops up, twitching her nose at the full-sized man on the grass. His hand snakes out and scoops her up.

"No!" Alex and I yell.

The screen door to the mudroom flies open. Still in her clothes from last night, Mom races out with Misti in her arms.

"What the hell is going on?" she cries.

Misti flops and kicks her way out of Mom's arms. Huffing and hissing, she bounds up to Wayne, opens her pink jaws, and bites his hand. He releases Little Gray along with a string of four-letter words. He winds back his foot, like he's going to kick Misti. I drop down to shield her with my arms.

Mom steps in between us, hands on hips.

"Get away from my children," she growls in a low, menacing voice I've never heard before.

Wayne freezes, jaw open, looking up at her as if he has no idea who she is. "But you said I could take the bunnies off your hands."

"I said no such thing. Leave my property before I call the police!"

He doesn't move.

Mom leans down and pushes him away from us, shoving his back and slapping his arms.

"Ow-owoo! Ow-owoo!" he cries as he scrambles to his feet. Brushing wet grass from his jeans, he gives me and Alex one last scowl, then turns and stumbles to the gate.

It slams shut behind him. Dropping to her knees, Mom takes us by the shoulders. Her breath smells of stale beer, her hair's a kinked-up mess, and the skin around her eyes is puffy. She opens her mouth to say something, but her chin trembles so much, it takes her a few tries.

"Are you both okay?" It comes out as a whisper.

We nod.

Tears spill down her cheeks and she pulls us to her, her whole body shaking with sobs.

"I'm sorry. I'm so sorry. How could I have let such a monster into my home? I've been a terrible mother. I-I need to get my act together. I'm going to send you two to your grandmother's. Just for a while, until I get myself straightened out. And I'll make sure Wayne can't ever come near us again. Things are going to change. I promise."

Alex and I twist our lips at one another. Neither one of us is convinced things will change all that much, but it's okay. We know she's trying, and I can tell Alex loves her for it just as much as I do.

"Can we bring the bunnies to Grandma's?" I point at the five tiny bundles of fur hopping around Misti.

Mom wipes the tears from her face and smiles. "Of course."

"Yeah, we can't leave the bunnies." Scooping up the gray one, Alex hands her to me. "I'm glad you went back for Little Gray."

"Her name's not *Little Gray*," I say, cupping her proudly to my cheek. "It's *Alice*."

———

Susan Conner is a lifelong writer and artist who has decided her mid-life mission is to spread kindness, healing, magic, and whimsy. Along with her two dogs, five cats, three barn cats, and a menagerie of other critters, she makes her home on a sprawling cattle ranch in southeastern Montana. In between emptying litter boxes and renovating the farmhouse her grandfather built, she paints, draws, creates digital art, and writes poetry and fiction for adults and young adults. Follow her on Twitter @SusansWordJar and at www.susanswordjar.com.

THE SILVER GIRL

―――――――――

CHARLOTTE A BOSTOCK

Aya should have left home far earlier. The rough brick exterior of the house rasped against her vest as she sidled up to the corner and peered around. Her tutor, Hilan, had arrived early and now stood at the door with Aya's mother, shaking his head with a familiar exasperated smile. The ranger adjusted the bow slung over his shoulder and stepped back from the door.

Aya pressed herself flat against the wall and waited for the thud of Hilan's receding steps. With luck, she could lose him, perhaps hide in the hills for the morning. *Maybe Keres is back in town . . .*

Hilan approached the corner instead. Aya darted behind the weedy bushes near the house and crouched low as his tall figure came into view between the foliage.

Go away, you relentless—

"Aya?" He scanned the yard and street, before giving up and striding away.

When reluctantly agreeing to apprentice with him, Aya hadn't expected such persistence. Her other tutors had known when to give up!

Leaving her sparse cover, she ran to the next house in a swift half-crouch, the dagger at her hip slapping against her leg. The village was well awake now, and from atop his roof, the thatcher rebuked her for running through his yard. Aya raised a hand and grinned. Passing a few more houses, she rejoined the packed-earth street with a cautious glance both ways.

Hilan walked at the far end. Hissing a quick curse, Aya ran in the opposite direction. She dodged fellow villagers and the transparent memory fragments dotting the street. The fleeting, incorporeal figures were oblivious to their own existence in the tangible world, and equally ignored by most folk. Aya needn't have dodged them, but it felt a little wrong to run *through* someone just because she could. She vaulted a stationary cart and rounded the next corner. *Almost there.*

At the house of Keres, the memory tracker, Aya pushed through the low gate, passing the picketed brown mare and her wagon in the next yard. She knocked on the dark blue door and threw a glance back down the street for Hilan. Silence in the house. Thick curtains were drawn behind true glass windows, clean and clear. She knocked again and the door swung open midway.

In age, Keres could've been someone's grandmother, and a formidable one at that. Her sharp blue eyes were ever scrutinising, grey hair pulled back high and secured in several thick braids. She raised one eyebrow and allowed a small smile at the corner of her mouth. "Back again, child?"

"It's Aya. I wondered if you had any tracking to do today? Do you need another pair of hands, perhaps?" Even an errand would be enough if it meant she could share Keres's company. "I could—"

A growly squawk interrupted from within the house and drew Keres away with a tut. Serpent-shaped talismans clinked in her braids.

"I'd love to help," Aya called into the gloomy interior. Keres had only lived in the village a year, and provided no formal apprenticeship, but Aya had offered her assistance half-a-dozen times regardless. The outcome hadn't yet changed from refusal, but nor did Keres seem bothered that Aya asked. It was enough to give her hope.

Keres returned with a small red dragon perched on her forearm. Spar, a wren-dragon, often circled the skies above the village, his red scales sparkling in the sunlight. He belonged to Keres, as all dragons belonged to someone. Those nearer to the size of hounds and horses were said to be immeasurably expensive, and anything larger belonged to legend.

"Thank you, child," Keres said, "but no. Spar is all I need." With a dismissive nod, she closed the door.

"She wouldn't want someone who gets so lost walking their own streets anyway," Hilan said behind her. "Forgot where the woods are again, did you?"

Aya raised her chin, arms crossed. "I thought *you'd* be in the woods by now."

"Not without my apprentice." Ignoring Aya's protests, he nudged her along the path and through the gate. "I wouldn't be much of a ranger if I couldn't find you hiding in the bushes, would I?"

She turned with a sigh and marched down the street ahead of her tutor.

He chuckled. "You're nothing if not tenacious, 'prentice."

"Yet hardly your apprentice by choice." She sidestepped a ghost-like memory of two young men laughing as they walked. "I haven't spent more than a month under your tutelage."

Hilan was, as ever, unperturbed. "Perhaps, but you'll not lose me so easily."

She looked skyward. *Clearly.* Undergoing study in the woodlands was intended to minimise distractions and keep Aya under control, something her village-wide family had failed to do her whole sixteen years. "And what if I don't want to watch plants grow? Or hunt game?"

"Come now, there's more to it than that. Last month I freed a wolf from a hunter's snare. She tried to bite my fingers off for it, of course." He flexed his right hand with a grimace.

"Won't the hunter be angry you interfered?"

"Let them. I wasn't going to leave the beast to die. It's part of the job, our job. Unless you'd rather follow Keres around like a lost kit instead?"

"I'd rather track memories with her. She goes on true adventures, you know. Beyond this place."

"Oh, *true* adventures." Hilan raised his brows in mock wonder. "I hadn't heard."

"Even you can't deny that solving mysteries with a dragon ally is more exciting than *anything* that happens in this valley."

"Indeed." He grinned and nudged her arm as he strode further ahead. "This way, 'prentice."

* * *

"Remember your anchor."

Kneeling in the woodland scrub, Aya drew the bowstring back until her thumb brushed her jaw. The yew curved gently in her grip, the draw weight light enough that she could hold the position with little strain.

Across the fern-scattered clearing, a crude round target leant against a tree just out of comfortable range. Hilan observed from her right, hands clasped behind his back, and murmured occasional instruction.

Archery was the only part of Hilan's tutelage that didn't numb her mind. For all that rangers could roam freely and even heal with magic, it took years of cataloguing mushrooms and hunting game to get there, and the occasional day of archery wasn't worth it to Aya.

She adjusted her aim with a steady exhale. Before she could let the bowstring slip free, a memory fragment passed through the clearing. The girl appeared silver-white and bled smoky residue with every movement. Aya lessened the tension on the bowstring as the girl paused and cast a skittish gaze across the quiet woodland.

"Aya?" Hilan prompted.

She pointed without looking away from the girl, for fear of losing her to a blink. That was all it took; a moment and they were gone. "Fragment," she murmured.

"Ah. Well, let it be. It'll move on soon."

"No, look. She's lingering."

Hilan approached to see from her angle. Placement mattered in viewing the fragments, but how to purposely find such a place, Aya had no idea.

"I see her," he said, straightening. "Now, let's get back to practice."

"Have you known them to stay visible so long?" Aya asked. She set the bow and arrow down, all focus given over to the memory.

Between hasty glances at the trees, the girl rummaged in a woven satchel at her side.

"I don't pay much attention to them," Hilan admitted. "They set me on edge a bit, seeing someone long-passed."

You sound superstitious, Aya chose not to say.

The girl stilled like a beast set to run, wide eyes scanning for some closing threat. The smoke of her movements dissipated in her stillness and revealed details Aya had never had the opportunity to see in a fragment before.

Though leached of colour, the girl appeared only a little older than Aya. Freckles spattered high cheekbones as darker grey spots on silver skin. One long braid hung over her shoulder, and—

The girl darted away.

Aya jumped to her feet, but the memory vanished past the crude target. "She ran!"

Hilan waved a hand. "Oh well— Aya! Where are you going?"

Aya charged after the girl she could no longer see, gripped with a sudden need to know if she had escaped her pursuer. Hilan's calls faded. Weaving through the trees, Aya glimpsed silver flashes, short bursts of the memory in motion.

Ahead, the girl tripped and tumbled to the ground. The contents of her satchel scattered, lost in a blur to the surrounding flora. She rolled over and flung a rock back. Aya dodged as the silver projectile flew past her head. The girl was up and running again, and gaining ground. Perhaps the rock had struck true and slowed the threat.

Aya burst into a clearing as something unseen pulled the girl down again. The residual smoke of her frantic struggle obscured her, hiding the threat.

Aya stared as the steady beat of worry built in her chest. The girl held up one hand, eyes wide and pleading. Silver tears shimmered on her cheeks, mouth open to scr—

Aya staggered back, breaking her visual with the memory.

Her pulse was thrumming, breaths quaking. She backtracked further and something barbed snapped around her leg. Aya let go a cry of shock as it yanked her down and the barbs dug in.

Aya twisted onto her back, fumbling for her knife. The rope-like thing wrapping her calf was lined with thorns and cinching tighter. She hacked with her blade, again and again until the creature couldn't retain its damaged grip.

At the first hint of freedom she scrabbled back, kicking to cover her retreat. Another crushing grip seized her arms and hauled her backwards. Rising panic clouded her brain. She could only think to fight, to struggle against the creature that . . . released her?

Hilan crouched protectively between her and the animated vines, a long blade in hand. He'd pulled her to safety.

"H-Hilan—"

"Are you all right?"

"Yes, I think." Aya hissed between her teeth as she pulled back her trouser leg. A dozen or more bloody punctures dotted her calf. "What is that thing?" She pushed herself up and found her wounded leg could bear weight.

More barbed ropes tore themselves out of the ground in a shower of displaced earth. They grappled the trees and ripped off branches as though trying to choke the life out of them. The ropes spread across the clearing, yet they all spawned from the same place in the churned-up ground. *Right where the girl fell.*

Hilan swapped his blade for his bow. "Run back to the village and warn the lord. Stop for nothing."

"What about you?"

Hilan loosed an arrow high as one of the ropes arced overhead. "I'm right behind you. Now run!"

He released another two arrows, one after another, at the woody centre of the mass, causing a violent, momentary constriction of the creature. Aya's mind protested leaving him, but her feet were already leading her away.

She ran through the scrub, whipped by ferns and branches, dodging and skipping over obstacles almost before she saw them. Down the hill into the valley, she nearly lost her footing and stumbled upright with a sick shock in her belly. She didn't slow, even when her feet pounded the packed earth of the village streets, when people shouted in her wake, she kept running.

* * *

After being denied admission to speak to the village landlord—and leaving a message with his disgruntled manservant instead—Aya ended up back at the woodland edge. Worry for Hilan spun its quiet poison into her thoughts and wrung into her fingers as she paced.

If he's hurt—if he dies—it'll be my fault. I ran off. I
—

Heavy steps crunched on the leaf litter, a merciful interruption. Hilan trudged down the slope.

"Hilan!"

He lifted one hand in tired acknowledgement, dropped his bow and sat down on the grass with a stiff groan. A bloody cut marred the side of his face, another on his forearm, and his arrow quiver was empty.

Aya knelt beside him. "Are you all right? What was that thing?"

Hilan winced as he gripped the cut on his arm. A soft light emanated from within his palm, paling his skin. He said nothing, jaw clenched, until he released his arm with a hard exhale. The cut was a faint scar now, as though years healed already. "That 'thing' was old magic. And I'll live. Is your leg all right?"

"It's—" Aya waved a hand impatiently. "Yes. What kind of old magic?"

"I've never seen it before, only read about its kind. There were malicious spirits in these hills a long time ago, before the mages came. They locked them away and made it safe for people to live here."

Aya sat back, took a moment with the information. "So . . . an angry ancient spirit just tried to kill us?"

"It seems so. Did you warn the lord?"

"His manservant wouldn't let me in, but he promised to carry my message."

"Ah." Hands on his knees, Hilan pushed himself up. "I best make sure it gets to him, then."

Aya stood, retrieving his bow, and together they started toward the village. Now that she knew Hilan was safe, she had room in her mind to contemplate the creature—the spirit—they'd encountered, and with Hilan's few words, her curiosity was piqued. "Maybe," she said as they came to the street, "it's angry because it's locked up."

"It is not our place to speculate," Hilan said, in a tone rather flatter than usual.

"Why not?"

"Because the mages would not have acted without good reason."

"Good reason," Aya muttered. For years she'd heard the same from tutors and townsfolk to explain the need for dancing and decorative needlework and everything in between. "It sounds convenient."

"It tried to kill you," Hilan pointed out incredulously. "And me."

"And the wolf tried to bite off your fingers."

Hilan's sigh was gravelly, and he said no more.

They garnered curious looks as they passed fellow villagers, but Aya's attention belonged elsewhere. Even the ghostly fragments on the street hardly caught her eye. "What else did your books say about this creature?"

"You want me to recite my studies?" Hilan dragged a hand down the side of his face. She'd never seen his temperament worn so thin. "Accounts with spirits mentioned violence, attacking settlers. That sort of thing."

"So, it's territorial?"

He took back his bow. "I'm sure it wasn't that simple. Still, this is beyond us. I need to seek the help of the mage guild."

"What about Keres?" Aya asked. "She could help, too."

"Aya." Hilan's voice held a rare edge of warning. "This is serious. This is not part of some adventure you seek."

"I know that. But a memory led me there, so it must have something to do with it. Keres can find out what really happened. Perhaps it'll help the mages."

Hilan shook his head, eyes briefly closed. "The mages are perfectly capable of tracking memories themselves. Now, you need to go home where it's safe."

He steered her forward with a hand on her back. She didn't protest again. Better to let him think her sullen. She set a little irked weight into her steps and folded her arms.

They parted ways near the landlord's house, but not before Hilan gave her an encouraging smile and reminded her that home was safest. It struck her then that whatever they'd faced had conjured fear in him for the first time since she'd known him. Now he was taking it upon himself to fix the problem of the spirit, to fix what Aya had uncovered.

But this isn't his responsibility. I'm the one who woke the spirit. Hilan hadn't even wanted to follow the memory . . .

She walked on, and only peeked over her shoulder once around the corner. Hilan was nowhere nearby. She turned away from the route home and backtracked furtively down the hill.

At Keres's house, she checked the street with more care than she had that morning, before running to the door and knocking.

"Please be home, please be home . . ." Bouncing on the balls of her feet, she knocked again, but a check around the yard confirmed the tracker was elsewhere. The pony and wagon were gone. In their place, wagon ruts and hoof prints compressed the dirt and led away from the house. Perhaps she'd gone on a job after all.

Aya followed the tracks at a conspicuously swift walk. Once the street met the main road out of the valley, she broke into a run, eyes on the tracks stretching ahead. Hilan would be furious, but trying to convince him would be little more than an exercise in argument.

Cresting a hill, she paused to catch her breath and swipe the sweat from her face. She scanned the gentle slopes and scattered woodlands with one hand raised against the sun. A small dark shape circled over the next valley. It could easily be mistaken for a hawk, but Spar's red scales flashed briefly in the light, and Aya was already on the move.

At the next crest, the small wagon on the roadside was a beacon of relief. The tracker herself knelt in the long grass.

"Miss Keres!"

"Aya?" She narrowed her eyes as Aya slowed near the wagon. "There is such a thing as too tenacious, child. Run back to your master. I told you, I don't need your help." Spar spiraled down from the sky and landed beside her.

Aya waded into the long grass. "But I . . ." She succumbed to the strain on her lungs and bent forward, hands on her knees, and dragged in several deep breaths.

Spar scratched the dirt with his clawed foot and snuffed the ground. Where he indicated, Keres began to dig with a small trowel.

Aya shook her attention away from their work. "I need your help."

"Oh yes, what for?"

"Hilan and I, we were in the woodlands and something attacked us. Hilan said it was magic, and he needed the mages' help to deal with it."

Keres grunted, still digging. "It sounds like Hilan has it under control, then."

"Except it was a memory fragment that led me to the magic. The girl I saw was involved somehow, I'm sure of it."

Keres finally looked up, brows raised. "And you think I can fix this?"

"I think you can find that memory and see what she did."

"I see." Keres snorted softly. "You might be right."

"So, you'll help?" Aya's relief spilled out in a laugh. "Thank you! I knew you—"

"First, we discuss payment."

Aya's shoulders dropped with her smile. "But . . ."

"I don't work for free." Keres shrugged and resumed digging.

Aya cast around as though something in the grassy hills would suffice as payment. She spread her empty hands. "I . . . I haven't anything of value. Nothing at all."

Spar squawked and a dull clinking answered Keres's excavation. She set the trowel aside and lifted the loose dirt in cupped hands. Sifting the earth between her fingers left three pieces of thick, dirty glass in her palms.

"My work leads to treasure often enough," she said, raising one of the pieces to the sun. Rough-edged and smudged, it looked like no special thing. "Whatever we find, I keep. And that'll be payment settled."

Aya nodded without pause. "Yes, agreed. Of course." She had no interest in treasures, only doing her part to set things right.

"Good." Keres dropped the glass into a pocket, retrieved her trowel and held an arm out for Spar. She straightened with ease. "Come then, girl. Let's find that memory."

* * *

Returning to the woodland required greater will than Aya had expected. Nerves tempered her eagerness to find the silver girl. She walked, alert to every crunch underfoot, to bird calls in the distance and tiny movements in her periphery. Knowing that spirit was out here somewhere made the whole forest seem a threat.

Keres and Spar followed quiet and close. The woman's impatience hovered at Aya's back in low sighs and murmurs to her dragon companion.

This isn't how a tracker thinks, Aya reminded herself. *Keres is not afraid.*

"Are you lost?" the woman asked quietly.

"No, it's not far," Aya whispered. She stepped around ferns encroaching on the faint path, and almost onto a black vine crossing the way. With a gasp, she backed into Keres. Spar squawked his indignation.

"What is it?" Keres demanded.

"Look there! I think that's it, that's the thing that attacked us."

Keres swept Aya back and wrenched a frond from the nearby ferns. She held it up to Spar, who promptly set it alight. The woman crouched, lowering the burning leaves close to the vine, and in the presence of fire, it cowered low into the earth.

Aya's stomach knotted. "It's spreading from where we found it."

Keres straightened, keeping the dwindling flames low. "Master Hilan's caution was not misplaced, but I do not think he'll be back with the mages in time to help us. This spirit could take our homes by then." She heaved in a breath, one hand on her hip in a pose of perfect disapproval. "It's up to us to deal with this now."

"*Us?*"

"Oh! I'm sorry, Aya, that was thoughtless," Keres said with an apologetic wince. "You've done well to show me the way. It's obviously not your responsibility to fix this. Perhaps you should return home, now. Be safe."

Aya recoiled from the sentiment, from abandoning the chance to prove her mettle. She shook her head, forced hardness into her voice. "I'm staying."

Keres grinned. "Good. Now show me this memory." Dropping the blackened leaves atop the vine, she gestured for Aya to lead the way.

They ventured wide, abandoning the faint path for low branches and prickly undergrowth instead.

"How will we deal with the spirit?" Aya asked.

"We must recage it."

So, she was of the same mind as Hilan, and likely the mages. Aya suppressed outward disappointment. "Are you sure?"

"I am. It's the only way to contain something with such power as this. But fear not, I've chanced upon one of these spirits before."

"How?" Aya couldn't quite hide the surprise in her voice. "Hilan said they were locked away centuries ago."

"Through memories. I'd thought that obvious."

Of course. Aya shook her head. *I have to find some way to apprentice with her.*

Keres had seen the spirit as close to firsthand as anyone could claim. Between them, she had the authority. At least until Hilan returned with the mages. And if she'd seen it before, if she knew safety lay in securing the cage . . .

Keres knows what to do.

"This is the place," Aya said as she stepped into the clearing where she'd practised archery that morning. She turned in a slow circle, scanning for suspect black lines. Nothing stood out of place. Not even the crude target she'd meant to shoot. "I was kneeling here, and the memory—the girl—she stepped out over there." She crouched in hopes of finding the silver apparition once more. "I can't see her now."

"You wouldn't if you saw her this morning," Keres said. "The time matters as much as your position, unless you have the right tools."

From within a leather pouch, she drew a handful of blue glass discs, each one ringed in gold metal casing.

A cleaned-up version of the dirty, rough glass Spar had found in the hills, Aya realised. Keres held them up to her eye in turn, testing different sizes.

"You can follow a memory with your eyes, as you've done," Keres said as Spar settled on her shoulder and peered at the glass. "But you have to keep up, and you'll lose them if you step wrong. These are hoarding lenses. Capture the memory in the glass and you can linger on details as long as you need, and follow as slow as you wish. No need to stand in the right place once it's captured, either."

A grin spread upon Aya's face. It was better than she'd expected. Not just tracking memories, but capturing them, studying them. "This is what you do as a tracker?"

"A slightly misleading title, but yes. It's not all adventures and excitement, mind. Some folk employ me simply to find something precious they've lost, and sometimes it's to solve murders, settle disputes. Each day is different."

"It sounds like a noble thing either way," Aya said. "I should like to do something noble."

"Well, here." Keres held out one of the smaller lenses. "No sense simply waiting on me. Look through."

Aya took the lens in both hands. It was heavy and smooth, the gold rings gleaming. She raised it to her eye and peered through the smoky blue glass.

And there she was. The girl stood exactly where Aya had first seen her, casting the same wary gaze across the surrounding woodland and clutching the woven satchel at her side. Subtle hints of colour accented the silver, enough to guess her hair was dark red, her clothes pale but stained.

Aya lowered the lens with a frown.

"Something wrong?" Keres asked.

"I think the girl dies at the end of this memory," Aya said. "I didn't watch last time, but seeing her again . . ." *Doesn't feel right.* She recalled Hilan's discomfort in seeing memories. People long-passed, he'd said.

"Ah." Keres nodded knowingly. "That's the danger with these. Some people—especially ones grieving or obsessed—get stuck watching memories if they're able to live them over and over. Properly made, these lenses are worth more than most folk will ever earn. In part due to rarity, and partly to keep that danger in check."

"Oh." Aya gripped the lens carefully at her words. She held it out to return but Keres gave a small shake of her head.

"You hold onto that for now." She returned her lenses to the pouch, keeping hold of only one. "Work with me today, Aya. It seems I may need another pair of hands this time."

"Truly?"

"Truly. Now, you follow the memory slowly, see if there's anything you missed the first time, and I'll go on ahead with Spar to make sure the way is safe. We'll see what we can learn."

Her words lightened Aya's heart. "All right! I'll—"

Keres held up a hand for silence. "The memory is captured in the glass now," she explained. "Walk with her, and she'll lead you along the events. Control the speed with the gold rings. It's somewhat intuitive, but you'll see."

"I will. Thank you! And be careful!"

"I'll be fine," Keres said as she raised a larger lens to her eye. After a moment, she pocketed it and set off past the archery target.

As Keres disappeared among the trees with Spar on her shoulder, Aya dropped a hand to her side, to the dagger that felt far too small now that she stood alone.

No. Working with Keres was finally a reality and she had to make the most of it. She had to be more than her fear. Aya took a steadying breath and lifted the hoarding lens to her eye.

The silver girl walked into the clearing and stopped to cast her skittish gaze across the trees. Aya sidestepped slowly, keeping the lens to her eye while trying to maintain balance. The girl remained in place, but Aya was able to see her from other angles and spy new details. Mussed hair, a tear in the seam of her shirt at the shoulder. Her unyielding grip on the satchel so tight it scrunched the material. One shoe missing. *How did I miss so much before?*

Aya tried twisting the gold rings circling the lens, and the girl moved off through the trees. She ran slow, like wading through deep water, until Aya adjusted the rings again. Such a strange sensation, controlling another's motion, whether they were real or not.

She followed in true time until the girl fell. Aya backtracked, twisted the rings, and studied the moment. The girl's foot snagged on a high root. She released the satchel to break her fall, but still she hit the ground with a hard crash, and the satchel contents scattered. Papers and some kind of token tumbled out, and the girl's hand closed on a rock.

She made no attempt at retrieving the items, despite the grip she'd had on the satchel. Aya stowed the lens and crouched down in the scrub. The paper would be long rotted, but the token had looked solid. She shifted plants and leaf litter, avoiding spiders, and keeping mindful of snakes waking for summer.

"It's as I feared, Aya," Keres called as she jogged back through the trees. "The spirit is gaining strength and ground. We must hurry. Did you find anything?"

"Not yet. I—"

"The memory is captured. We can study it somewhere else in safety. Come." Keres charged past, hardly a glance at Aya kneeling in the scrub.

"How are we supposed to handle this if it's growing stronger?" She hurried to follow the surprisingly swift woman.

"We are going to find the cage before the spirit breaks completely free. It must have a lock or two still in place, else it would've wreaked havoc all over the region by now."

"But you and Hilan both said it has been caged with magic. How are *we* to fix that?"

Keres threw her an irritated glance. "I didn't say we need magic to fix it, did I? The magic is *in* the cage *and* its key. As long as we find both, we can secure the spirit."

A key. Aya turned halfway back to the area where the girl had fallen. "Keres, wait. The girl dropped something in the memory, over here." Aya jogged back and crouched down where she'd been searching. "Somewhere here . . ." She ran her hands along the ground, crawling further into the undergrowth.

"Spar, search," Keres said from the path.

The wren-dragon dropped down beside Aya and scratched the earth with his claws, snout down. She didn't know if he understood what he sought or indeed how, but his actions seemed as purposeful as her own. He beat his wings and screeched as he had when seeking the hoarding glass for Keres, and his insistence showed Aya where to dig.

She swept aside coarse leaf litter to the soft rotting layer beneath, disturbing crawling, burrowing insects. There amongst the natural debris, the carved token was wedged in the earth. As she reached for it, a black vine snapped up out of the dirt.

With a shout, Aya snatched up the token. The vine lashed at her, scraping her hand before Spar clamped burning jaws down on its barbed length. With a savage rip, he tore it in two.

The severed end dropped without a twitch, while the living length recoiled into the earth. Aya retreated to the path with Spar trotting at her feet before any more threats could surface.

"You found something?" Keres asked.

Aya held out the token as she and Keres fell into step, strides swift. The rectangular stone fit well in her palm. Discolouration told of its time lying forgotten in the dirt, but could not completely hide the grey symbols on its front.

"That's it," Keres whispered. "That's the key. Well done, Aya." She took it in hand.

The pale stone was woven with silver in some hybrid creation Aya had never seen before. Keres had said both the cage and key were made with magic, after all. The tracker rubbed her thumb over the symbols and the dull, dirty silver gleamed.

"I've seen that kind of marking before," Aya said. "On the ruins in the hills to the west. Maybe the cage is hidden there too."

"There's no structure in those ruins, nowhere to hide such a thing."

"It's breaking down, but there are markings like this all over the place. They're the same, I'm sure of it."

Keres shoved the key into her pocket. "All right. The ruins." Spar screeched as if in agreement.

"We should tell Hilan," Aya said. "The mages—"

"We don't need them," Keres snapped. "And we don't have time." She spun to face Aya, forcing her to back up before they collided. "I'll not discuss it further. Decide whether you are in this, or go home."

Aya nodded, unsure that Keres actually wanted an answer. The woman walked on.

Spar screeched again. He'd saved her, and Aya finally had a true chance to learn from Keres, to do good.

Of course I'm in this.

* * *

Enormous slabs of stone scattered the hills in the west, cracked and weathered, pillars toppled. Playing there as a child, Aya had imagined citadels and towers worth conquering. More recently, the ruins sufficed as worthy hideouts from her tutors.

She picked her way through the crumbling, ancient structures with familiar ease, Keres at her side and Spar circling overhead in the afternoon glare. Aya leapt onto a square slab at the crest of a hill. Only two of the support pillars still stood, while the crumbled remains of the rest lay engulfed by encroaching grass. The standing pillars displayed symbols similar to those on the key. Keres inspected them with narrow-eyed scrutiny.

"Yes," she muttered finally. "The cage must be near . . ." She dug the large hoarding lens out of her pocket and raised it to her eye. Keres surveyed the hills before stepping off the stone slab and down into the tall grass. Aya followed as a silent shadow, content to watch the woman at work, and take note of her techniques.

Keres—or the memory she followed—took them to a thin valley where boulders and chunks of ruins were wedged tight, long displaced by a landslide. She hauled herself atop the rock pile. "There's a cave over here. Well hidden." She gestured to a branch on the ground, about an arm-span long. "Bring that."

Aya retrieved the branch and followed as Keres moved on. Her agility took her ahead, while Aya traversed the boulders with careful avoidance of cracks that seemed made for trapping ankles.

She caught up where the rocks crushed against the hillside and almost completely hid a dark tunnel into the slope. In all her time playing in the hills, Aya had never seen it before.

Keres ventured into the dark without pause.

Aya swallowed. She squashed misgivings about mysterious dark caves with her clenched fists, and followed the tracker's lead.

She slipped down into the mouth of the tunnel, her footing all but sacrificed on the decline until she stumbled onto flat ground at the base.

Only a slice of sunlight reached into the cave with them. Whatever lay ahead, lay in darkness.

She glanced back up the slope. *Haven't gone too far yet. We could still get help. The mages. Hilan.* Beside her, Keres broke the branch against her knee. *But I am in this.*

"Can we light that?" she asked.

Keres shook her head. "Not yet. It's a long cave, I suspect, and these won't last long as torches." She tucked the broken branches under one arm and produced the hoarding lens once again. "This way."

She set off with the large lens held not to her eye for guidance, but far forward. As the darkness deepened the glass emitted a soft glow, enough to guide them through the ancient cave. Packed rubble walls held aloft a ceiling they couldn't see. Debris littered the path and the flagstone flooring was cracked underfoot.

Aya stuck close to Keres, who led with easy strides. She never paused to investigate or weigh forked options, ignoring divided paths as often as she traversed them. Spar, flying overhead, was lost to Aya's sight. Only an occasional soft squawk placed him above.

She couldn't say how far or long they walked. Time skewed in the dark, in the pit of nerves growing in her belly. Debris shifted underfoot and she found herself gripping the dagger handle for some chance at reassurance.

Some time later, Keres held out an arm to halt, and whispered without turning, "This is the place. The cage lies ahead. Ready?"

Aya's deep breath was shallower than she wanted. *Can't turn back now.* She shook out her hands and nodded. "Yes. Let's go—"

Keres caught her arm when she started forward. "Remember, whatever happens, we *must* lock the cage."

"I know." Aya winced at the woman's bony fingers pinching her arm. *Doesn't know her own strength.* "I understand. Well, I don't understand *how* . . ."

Keres released her with a grunt. She pocketed the lens and held out the branches. "Spar, light." Perched on her shoulder, Spar ignited the sticks with a spurt of flame.

Light flung wide and the surrounding tunnel took on a wavering, orange hue. Heavy shadows at the edges were eager to close in.

They stood before an arched entrance to a larger chamber beyond. Few details were discernible, save for heaped rubble and tangled black vines covering the floor. Aya clamped down on her shock, instinct taking her a few steps back.

"Keep the fire low," Keres said, handing Aya the smaller burning branch. "And step with care."

Aya swore under her breath and followed. Under the flames, the black ropes quivered but didn't move to attack. Compared to Keres, Aya's steps were excessively careful. She placed her feet as though balancing atop a thin wall, breath trapped tight in her chest.

"Worry not," Keres whispered. "They fear the fire, and they won't sense us with a little distance."

"I'm trying . . ." A glance up swallowed her words.

A stone dome arced over the vast chamber, held up by four square pillars. The barbed ropes wrapped and crushed the architecture and laced across the ceiling as though they held it up. Gaps between the black lines showed glimpses of the same silver symbols.

Ancient weapons hung along the side walls—black swords and stone hammers, cracked shields. Raised upon a wide stone platform at the back, stood a metal grid, as tangled and choked with barbed ropes as the rest. The metal shimmered softly, all but the right-most side of the cage aglow. A great mound of the vines covered the cage floor.

"We're near your first encounter with the spirit," Keres murmured. "Perhaps right beneath it."

Aya refused the retreat her body wanted. She squeezed the torch, and jumped as Spar fractured the silence with a high screech.

Keres pinched his snout shut too late. A great shudder passed through the chamber, rumbling like thunder. Dust sifted from the ancient architecture and the mound in the cage shifted. Whatever lay trapped rose up, straining against the restraints.

"Aya, get back."

She hardly noticed Keres pulling her to the far side of the chamber, staring instead at the creature emerging from its barbed bonds.

It scraped itself against the metal bars and severed a handful of ropes with a snap. Silver-blue scales gleamed where the ropes fell away. A horned snout tore free. The creature's massive head swung around and with a gaping fanged maw it clamped down on the bonds.

"Th-that's—is that—" Aya wrestled for words. "It's a dragon."

"Their spirit, their soul—whatever you wish to call it," Keres said with an unexpected edge of contempt. "This here is a violent creature. It cannot leave this place. Free, it would incite violence in all its dragon kin."

Spirit though it was, the dragon thrashed against the cage with terrifying, tactile ferocity. The ropes on the chamber floor receded, coiling back through the bars, and wrapped the dragon's body anew. Those on the ceiling and pillar did not move.

"These ropes, they're not part of the spirit at all," Aya said. "They're part of the cage, aren't they?"

"Meant to subdue," Keres said with a nod. She took Aya's burning branch and wedged it into an ancient sconce on the wall.

Then Hilan's studies were wrong about the spirit, and its cage. She wondered what else had been taught as truth all these years. Over the crash and growl of the dragon came high-pitched clinks of something hitting the flagstones. Aya peered into the gloom. Glass?

Not glass. Dragon scales.

Scraping itself against the cage had torn them off. As the scales hit the ground, they crystallised, and the clear silver grew cloudy.

Hoarding lenses. Keres's treasure. She grabbed the woman's arm. "Look—"

"Later, later. This way, now," Keres said, pulling free. "I'll show you where to place the key."

"Me?"

"You're more agile than I, and Spar will have a hard time fitting the key with his claws. Come, see atop the cage? There are two locks and only one remains intact. The other needs this key to reseal the magic completely." She gestured at the slabs of scattered rubble. "This mess used to be a bridge, so you'll have to climb, but the cage bars are safe to touch, I assure you. Come, now." Flaming stick in hand, Spar on her shoulder, Keres set off toward the cage.

Aya trailed more slowly. ". . . How do you know all this?"

Memory, obviously.

She stopped in her tracks. Since they'd entered the chamber, Keres hadn't once raised a lens to her eye to investigate. She hadn't shown awe at their surroundings, not even at the giant, raging spirit of a dragon. Only contempt.

She's been here before.

Eyes squeezed shut, Aya dug her nails into her palms. *Of course. She knew the way, knew the treasure she'd find.* Aya had been so enthralled with following memories and learning the mechanics of the hoarding lenses . . .

She still had the one Keres had lent her, a tempting weight in her pocket now. She drew it out, turned it once, twice. She'd looked aside from a memory once. This time she had to see to the end.

Through the blue glass, the chamber appeared much the same, with its collapsed bridge and rubble strewn floor. A smoky apparition of the dragon lay over the real one's struggle, while the vines, still wrapping much of its body, were calm and contained within the cage. Both locks must still have been in place back then.

A ghostly Keres and Spar crossed the chamber a few steps ahead of the physical pair. And at the base of the cage stood the girl, the silver girl who'd started it all. She gripped an axe in one hand, blade pointed toward Keres. She held the other through the bars with her palm pressed against the dragon's snout as though reassuring the spirit.

The real Keres glanced back and stalled when she saw Aya holding the lens to her eye. "What are you doing?"

Aya lowered the glass. A hardness settled in her stomach. "You were the hunter in the memory, weren't you?"

Keres's face creased in a frown. "What are you saying, girl?"

"I'm saying you lied. You've been here before. You knew that girl."

"Aya. This is *clearly* not the time." Keres gestured at the cage. "We have a dragon to—"

"Trap?" Aya offered. "What's to say you're not lying about this spirit, too? Maybe it doesn't need to be here at all. Maybe you only care to keep Spar docile and digging up your wealth!"

"All right." Keres held one hand out in a vaguely placating gesture. "Yes, I knew what lay here. But I never lied about the consequence of setting this spirit free. We *will* lose control of dragons. You're not a stupid girl, are you? Surely you see the sense in obedient beasts over vicious ones."

"But do you have any *proof?*"

Keres raised her brows. "I don't have to *prove* anything, especially not to a child."

"Well . . ." Aya searched for some reasoning Keres could not deny. She gestured at Spar perched on her shoulder. "Don't you care that Spar has no choice?"

"I care about helping *people*," Keres said. "That is my work. You called it noble, remember?"

Aya stared. "Did you help that girl?"

"*Enough*," Keres snapped. "Now get over here—"

"No. I will not move until you admit what you did!"

"It was *not* me." Keres stabbed a finger at her own chest and inhaled sharply. "*I* couldn't keep up with her. But I was not alone."

Not . . . Disbelief pummelled Aya's understanding. She looked to Spar perched on Keres's shoulder and realised the tracker was never alone. Aya shook her head, groped for words. ". . . Spar? *He* was the hunter?"

"He was only meant to retrieve the key," Keres said mildly. "Her death was unintended, but she'd left me little choice."

"You *made* him attack her." Aya's belly gave a sick twist. "Why? Who was she to you?"

"My last meddling apprentice. She ran a little too wildly on the same nobility you admire so much. Be careful with that. Still, it was lucky I stayed local; I had no idea where this key ended up, nor the memory, until you sought my help."

That's why you turned up a year ago. A ripple of anger played catch-up as facts fell into place.

"Now I have a chance to fix what she did," Keres went on. "I should thank you for that."

"Do *not* thank me." Aya ground the words out, never more furious. Never more humiliated.

The woman closed the space between them to a couple of strides.

"Why did you bring me here?" Aya asked, stepping back. If she ran now, Spar would chase her down long before she made it out of the tunnels. "You had the key. You didn't need my help."

"Because you're stubborn, child!" Keres threw her hands up. "Pounding on my door every other day. I knew you'd never let things be, just like the girl before you. But where she failed, you can be more. Help me today, do the right thing, and I'll give you the apprenticeship you seek. You can even keep that lens. There's plenty more here."

In need of no contemplation, Aya tossed the glass at Keres's feet. "I won't be bought."

"Then I have no use for you."

Keres hurtled the burning branch at Aya's head. She dodged clumsily and the stick clattered onto the flagstones.

"Spar, go!" Keres held out the key and Spar grasped it with his clawed feet. "Lock the cage!"

He launched into flight. Aya shoved past Keres and lunged after him. Her hands brushed his barbed tail and she recoiled at the sting of cuts on her fingers. Spar soared across the chamber toward the top of the cage, well out of reach in moments.

Aya cast around for something she could use to stop him. She recoiled at the thought of hurting the wren-dragon, but the armoury of ancient weapons lining the walls was the only advantage she could see.

She ran to the far side of the chamber and wrenched down a silver and stone mace, a magic-forged hybrid like the key. It clunked onto the flagstones, heavier than she'd anticipated.

"You can't stop him!" Keres called.

It's not over. Not yet. There's still a second lock!

She'd witnessed Keres use her control over Spar to do her bidding, to seek her wealth, and now to kill. It was more than enough proof that she had to be stopped.

As the wren-dragon flew into position over the cage, Aya ran to the base of the stone platform. The vines no longer wrapped the bars, instead focusing all their attention on trapping the thrashing dragon within. With both hands Aya threw the mace onto the platform and followed, hauling herself up a height equal her own. She straightened cautiously, a yard from a creature ripped out of legend, larger than any house or hall.

She couldn't let it shake her, and she hadn't the time to marvel. Spar was out of sight on the far side of the cage. He'd be moments from replacing the key.

Nerves thrumming madly, Aya reached a hand to the cage. Her fingers closed around the metal. The silver shimmer from the bars bled painlessly onto her skin, and the magic vibrated, coursing through the metal into her grip.

"Aya!" Keres was at the base of the stone platform. Her shout broke Aya's fixation with the magic and urged her onward.

Hauling a mace made the ascent awkward, helped not at all by the height and the screaming dragon and Keres climbing in pursuit. Muscles straining, she gritted her teeth all the way to the top.

Aya dragged herself onto the flat of the cage, knuckles aching in her death grip. Refusing to look down, she sought Spar on the far side instead. He gripped the bars with hooked wingtips as he tried to manoeuvre the key into the open lock with his teeth and talons.

Hauling the mace, gritting her teeth, Aya crawled toward the secure lock on her side.

A large metal square, surrounded by webs of shimmering silver, housed an identical key stone to Spar's, with metal claws holding it in place. The symbols on the key glowed silver-white. She reached a hand toward it cautiously and the glow brightened. The air around it buzzed, her fingers tingling. She withdrew her hand.

Aya hefted the silver-stone mace over her shoulder. If she couldn't break it, she'd have to go after Spar.

Please don't let it come to that.

The dragon spirit slammed itself against the cage again, dropping Aya to her knees with a quake through the metal. It snapped long jaws at ropes coiling into the top of the cage and tore them back down in pieces.

Aya planted her feet where the bars crossed. Steeling herself with quick breaths, she swung the mace down at the intact lock with all her strength.

A shock of power surged into her hands and up her arms, every nerve singing. She held tight to the weapon, groaning through a clenched jaw. Keres's call barely registered. Aya swung the mace again. The key cracked.

"Aya!" Keres pulled herself onto the cage. "Stop!"

Aya gritted her teeth. Swung again.

And the key shattered.

Stone and steel flew, and Keres tackled Aya too late. The mace clattered between the bars and disappeared into the seething fight between dragon fangs and barbed vines below. The silver shimmer on the cage flickered and faded.

"You wretch!" Keres shouted. "What have you done?"

Below, the dragon abandoned its fight with the ropes and swung its attention to the bars with new focus.

Aya gasped. She shoved at Keres. "We have to get off the cage! Go!"

With a glance at the dragon, Keres swung herself over the edge of the cage and descended, and Aya scrabbled to follow. The dragon below hooked its claws into the bars. Bending metal groaned in reluctant surrender.

Aya clambered down too fast with numb fingers, feet slipping, metal shuddering. She lost her grip and fell the last few yards, landing awkwardly on the edge of the stone platform. She rolled off and crashed onto the chamber floor.

Splitting metal screamed under the dragon's strength as it tore open an exit. It climbed out halfway, and a rope lashed its hind leg. Snarling as though it had finally lost its patience, the dragon rounded back. It clamped its jaws over a concentrated mass of ropes on the cage base with a crunch, threw its head back and tore the roots of the parasitic vines out of the floor.

The remaining vines ceased their motion. Where they bound tight to architecture, they crumpled and withered. Mortar crumbled where their presence must have been integral. Clutching her bruised torso, Aya grimaced at the dying tendrils peeling away from the domed ceiling. Fine dust stung her eyes. The massive stones began to shift, and specks of sunlight pierced the dark. A terrible weight sunk in her stomach.

What have I done?

She dragged herself back, teeth clenched against the pain. The first chunk of ceiling stone slammed onto the floor and a full burst of sun burned into the chamber. Aya made to rise, staggered. The dragon stepped down into the chamber with a quake through the floor and the force dropped her. She curled around an onslaught of fear, as one scaled forefoot compressed the flagstones an arm's-length away.

Snout to tail, the dragon spirit appeared bulky with muscle, yet nothing but crystalline silver scales made up its form. The spiked end of its tail curled back around to fit the width of the chamber.

Crouching low, the dragon spread vast wings overhead. The silver scales across its body hardened, and the wings lost their translucency as a hailstorm of stone and earth pummelled down. Aya couldn't move for space, awe or terror, emotions fighting for priority. Close enough to feel the vibration of the dragon's deep growl, she could've brushed its underside scales had she simply reached out, but her limbs were rigid.

The clamour of raining rubble gradually ceased. Brick and dirt tumbled off the dragon's back as it straightened. Whole trees and flora had fallen in with the ceiling, and a pale orange dust cloud now veiled the chamber.

Aya heaved in a breath. She rolled over, coughing on the dust, and crawled a few paces clear of the dragon. Keres crouched near the tunnel entrance with not a scratch for her troubles, while Spar fluttered down to settle on the newly-fallen rubble.

He screeched, snapping his wings wide and drawing the spirit's attention. It inspected its diminutive wren-kin in silence, black eyes unblinking, its judgement passed with a snort of smoke.

The dragon straightened. Air gusted beneath its wings as it took flight toward the broken ceiling. Aya retreated stiffly, blinking against the gale of dust. Horns and talons tore the dome wider and rained more debris upon the wreckage below. Then, with a roar that reverberated through Aya's chest, the dragon dragged itself to freedom.

The silence in its wake settled slowly. She straightened with a wince, gripping her side. Despite the destruction, the pain in her ribs, and consequences as yet unknown, she looked upon the dragon's cage without regret. Nothing deserved a fate of such suffering.

Beside her, Spar let go a mournful cry toward the gaping ceiling.

Somewhere beyond the dust cloud, a human voice called back. Aya cast around, but the source was indiscernible, the words too muffled to understand. "Did you hear that?"

"Spar," Keres said, ignoring her. "Here." She held out one arm. The wren-dragon cocked his head. "*Here.*"

Spar raised his snout to the distorted sky. He crouched and leapt, beating his wings into flight. The dust cloud swallowed his shape with a last muffled squawk.

"Spar!"

Aya winced at the crack in Keres's shout. The woman's shoulders dropped, before she turned on Aya and raised an accusing finger. "You did this. You took my dragon from me!"

"He wasn't yours to begin with," Aya said. She heard the folly, and the fact. "I-I just set him free."

"Oh, such *wit*." Keres pulled her dagger and advanced. Aya matched her steps back with both scuffed hands raised. Her boot crunched on crystallised dragon scales. "You and that girl, both meddling, both playing the vigilan—"

A loud shout preceded an audible whoosh. The dust whipped into a spiral and flew from the room through the gaping ceiling.

"Drop the knife, Keres!"

Aya raised an arm against the blaze of crisp sunlight and squinted at the glaring patch of blue, dragon-less sky. The silhouettes of several people stood around the edge of the hole, trees towering at their backs.

"Hilan?" Her eyes adjusted to find his features, as well as the bow he aimed at Keres. Aya recognised the women and men around him as mages, marked by the coiling green guild bands on their biceps, and pale glowing auras in the hands of two.

"Which one of you released the spirit?" One of the mages called sharply.

"Whatever happened," Hilan cut in, "we'll settle it. Just put the dagger down, Keres."

"And let a *criminal* go free?" Keres called back, plenty of shock in her tone. A mirthless smile crossed her face as she raised her brows at Aya. "Only you can make sure this ends peacefully. Turn yourself in. They were coming here to secure the spirit too, so you better tell them *you* set it free."

Two of the mages knelt at the edge of the hole with taut hands focused toward the rubble in the chamber. Piece by piece, stones rolled across the floor to form the first steps of an ascending staircase, metal clanging into place on the sides.

End it peacefully? Either she attacks me or Hilan attacks her, or . . .

Aya exhaled a spiral of bad options. Keres wasn't wrong; the truth was the only card Aya carried, but a half-truth was no use to anyone. She nodded to Keres. "I won't lie. I'll tell them everything I did. And . . . everything you did."

"Listen, you brat," Keres said with a jab of the dagger at empty air. "You're in no position to argue."

"No, but Hilan's arrow isn't pointed at me," Aya said. Keres's gaze flicked up to him and back. "The mages are going to find out the truth whether or not I tell them. There's no point fighting. So . . ." She kicked a couple of dragon-scales forward with a scuff of her boot. They clinked across the broken flagstones. "Why don't you take your treasure and go? That's the only way I see this ending peacefully."

Keres raised narrowed eyes from the glass to Aya. "A head-start?"

Aya shrugged. "Call it what you like. I can hardly stop you if you choose to run."

Keres eyed Hilan and the mages above. Their stairs were halfway toward the ceiling already. Without relinquishing the point of her blade, she lowered to collect the offered scales, groping the rubble-strewn floor until she found them. Straightening, she scoffed and stepped back slowly. "There might be some hope for you yet, girl."

* * *

At the woodland edge, Aya paced with unexpected impatience leading her steps. Hilan had been gone from the village nearly a week helping the mages investigate the release of the long-gone dragon spirit. Having willingly given over her memories, they'd left Aya well enough alone, despite their furious disapproval of her actions. And while Hilan had backed her, a fortune in dragon scales seemed the greater balm for the mage guild.

He finally approached the woodland with the dawn-lit village at his back, and raised a hand in greeting.

She folded her arms in mock disapproval. "Did you forget where the woods are again, Master Hilan?"

"No." He shrugged the smaller of two bows off his shoulder and held it out. "I backtracked for this."

It was her own, thought lost after first chasing the girl in the memory. Aya dropped her arms. "How did you know I'd be here? We haven't spoken for a week."

"I saw your tracks."

Of course. She took the proffered bow with a nod of thanks. Then, "Did you find Keres?"

Hilan shook his head. "Not yet. It may take the mages some time. Keres is clever, after all." Hilan regarded her with mock scrutiny. "So, you got your adventure. What are you going to do now?"

"I hoped you wouldn't mind some company," she said. "And . . . I am sorry for the trouble I caused."

He clapped her shoulder. "You were trying to do right."

"And I'd like to do more," Aya said, before reeling in her enthusiasm. She cleared her throat. "But properly this time. I want to learn. A ranger's skills could help me do some good in this world."

"Oh, I see." Hilan nodded. A grin pulled at his mouth as he started into the trees. "Well then, 'prentice. Let's get to work."

———

Charlotte A. Bostock is a lifelong SF/F writer from Australia. Her works are primarily dark fantasy, with hard magic systems and characters who are more than a little rough around the edges. When she isn't writing, Charlotte can be found photographing planets, restoring typewriters, or working through an ever-growing to-be-read list. Charlotte can be found on Instagram @CharlotteABostock, Twitter @cabostockauthor or at www.charlotteabostock.com.

Outfoxing the Fox

Mei Davis

My first glimpse of England was of rain. But it was nothing like the god-kissed sun-shower that had bathed my wedding. Neither was it the brief yet heavy hammer that battered the shores of my homeland during monsoon season.

This English rain was an endless grey shroud, cloaking all and sundry in an incessant, dreary drizzle as we disembarked from the ocean liner, my arm tucked within my new husband's as he led me down the gangplank and onto the damp streets of my new country.

My newest con.

"Always so rainy?" I asked in a birdlike voice.

"That's England, darling," Edward replied with a dimpled smile. "But never fear. You'll be my bit of sunshine, and I'll be yours." He was the type of young man who looked exactly his age, and acted a great deal younger. His trim form fit snugly into an expensive suit, and while his tie was askew and jacket hopelessly creased, his carefree style went glove in hand with the windswept shock of hair that fell in pleasant waves over a pair of deep blue eyes, faintly pulsing with the hungry naivety of youth.

He leaned down and kissed my cheek. I blushed

and giggled stupidly. The pedestrians milling about the dingy, chockablock streets of London port, both well-to-do and plebeian alike, began to stop and stare. Men appraised me from beneath the brims of their Trilbys and wool caps. Children drowned in dour coats tugged at their nannies' sleeves and pointed. Women screened their passing whispers behind gloved hands.

I took it all in with a smile. No matter where I go, I rather like being a spectacle, grand entrances and all of that, and despite Edward's purchase of Western-style clothing, I'd insisted on making my Atlantic debut in a splashy red silk *kimono*, embroidered with gold cranes and trimmed with a traditional *obi* sash and a pair of tottering *geta* sandals.

Yet it wasn't merely my clothing that had arrested every eye. Make no mistake, I'd worked extremely hard on this form, and was particularly proud of it. For weeks, I'd studied European magazines and portraiture, until I could fashion exactly the sort of woman who could please men from both sides of the hemisphere: a diminutive figure, the perfect amalgam of western and eastern facial features, and long, unbound hair that shone like a sheet of black ice down my back.

My work spoke for itself. I was a bright, exotic bird amidst the flock of these drab sparrows, and if they looked at me, it was with a shade of desire; if they whispered, with the taint of jealousy.

Two porters with umbrellas approached out of the gawking crowd. One of them positioned an umbrella over us, while the other touched his cap and spoke:

"We've got the luggage in the motor, my Lord." He gave me a quick bow. "My Lady."

My Lady. Like music to my ears.

Edward patted my hand. "Shall we, Kyoko darling? Claybury Castle awaits!"

We followed the men to the Rolls Royce parked along the curb, I with little mincing steps upon my platform sandals, and my sister with steady, even strides in her practical yet hideous boots as she trailed several steps behind. Niko bore my traveling case and a perpetual frown, and any remnants of her youth or vibrancy were consumed by a brown, high-necked frock. Although I could forgive her the demure apparel —she was, after all, taking on the role of my lady's maid —I could not look past her other choices. A forgettable face. A doughy body. A swath of dull hair that neither glossed nor shimmered in the sun. Since our creation, Niko had been the kind of dumplings-over-flowers Kitsune which I abhor. What sort of shapeshifter neither flaunts their looks for praise, nor abuses their power for gain? Gives us all a bad name.

As Edward and I settled into the backseat, she took her place up next to the chauffeur, then turned around to speak to me in Japanese:

"Well Kyoko, you've got every eye on you, just as you like."

"Just as I deserve, you mean."

"Another year, another husband."

"Variety is the spice of life—especially when one's lifetime numbers in the millennia."

"But why Edward? You had your pick of shallow, thick-headed men at home in the Land of the Rising Sun, yet you insisted on luring in this creature you call an Earl, and accompanying him back to his homeland."

"'Even the bugs eat knotweed', as the say." I

caressed Edward's shoulder. He didn't speak a lick of Japanese, and watched our conversation with a blissful smile. "You may not understand, but I have a great weakness for these gentle, imbecilic souls."

"Don't pretend as if you actually like him." She leveled me with a fierce stare. I may be the master potter of the family, molding my victims to my will, but Niko is the master miner. There's little she can't unearth with her prying, pickax ways. "What is it you truly seek, Kyoko? Did you really travel all the way to the other side of the globe simply so you could put another notch in your *obi*?"

"While I appreciate how crude you make it all sound, this is much more than merely another conjugal conquest. I've outfoxed enough shoguns. I can reel in those old fools without even trying. 'A frog in a well cannot know the depths of the sea'. How could I possibly plumb the depths of mankind's stupidity when confined to one continent alone? It was high time for a change of scenery. To see the world, to meet new people. And what better place to start than with a banal little island, full of nothing but absurd politeness, uncomfortable formal wear, and rigorous tea drinking?"

"Yes," Niko deadpanned, "completely different from Japan."

"I needed a new challenge, and these Englishmen —" I lavished Edward with a treacly smile, "—think they're so very, very clever. Needed taking down a peg, you know."

"Oh, I do know," Niko replied, and with a pointed smirk not to my liking. "And I suppose the fact that you'd be the first Kitsune to ever do it played no part in your decision."

"What can I say, I'm a glutton for bragging rights."

I blew my new husband a kiss. He reciprocated in kind, his gaze unadulterated in its devotion. Yes, I'd certainly snagged myself a big prize. Even two oceans away, Edward Caravelle, the sixth Earl of Ashbourne, was famous for his obnoxiously vast wealth. No doubt every girl with a dream and a pair of eyelashes had batted up to him at some point, and I imagined with relish the gossip that no doubt raged upon the news of his marriage to an unknown, foreign chit. *First they come home with American brides, and now this? What does he mean by marrying this oriental creature? Heavens, but does she even speak English?*

Little did they know that I did indeed speak English, and every other language besides. Little did they guess that behind the guise of this beautiful, simpering cherry blossom lived a most ancient and foxy trickster: the feared and revered Kitsune, devourer of men's souls.

And oftentimes their pocketbooks.

The chauffeur finished stowing the luggage in the boot, cranked the engine to life, and we sped towards Claybury Castle as a Ryu, those mighty dragons of old, flies towards its glittering, purloined hoard.

* * *

"The very soul of England," Edward enthused as the motor hummed through Leicester. He gestured to the window, where emerald grasses dotted with clouds of bleating sheep flitted quickly past. "The countryside has stood for centuries as a preserving rockbed of

English culture and mores. Peace and tranquility writ large in the boundless pastures and quaint thatched-roofed villages. Here, the time-honored traditions that make these lands a jewel among nations are kept alive and well: angling and cricket, fetes and hunts, and the bucolic lifestyle of the country."

These were the dullest hours of my centuries-long remembrance, nothing but a homogenous blend of herds, hedgerows, and his patriotic harangues.

"My heart proud to be Englishwoman," I said to him, then said to Niko in Japanese, "and my mouth gags to say it."

"I find his passion refreshing," she replied, "and even you must admit the views are charming, in their way."

"If I was after grasslands and sheep, I would have gone to Mongolia. This fool thinks he knows all about his precious England, but fails to see what's right in front of his face."

For Edward was only partially correct. The countryside may indeed be the soul of England, but not in the way he believed. Though the industry of man may have eroded its presence, beyond the cement and metal of the cities, another world thrives. One not merely of the natural, but the preternatural, populated by those peculiar beings spoken of in chilling tones, passed down through ancient scrolls and children's bedtime stories. In Japan they are called *mononoke*. In England they go by fairy or fay, angel or demon.

But in any language and by any name, their essence remains the same: phenomenon that cannot be explained, creatures that are to be feared. The denizens of the spiritual realm of which Niko and I claim our citizenship.

"Look at that that, Niko." I inclined my head to the window, where green, humanoid wisps the size of my thumb battled in the pasture. "Peace and tranquility, he says, when those grass sprites are having an outright war. And that lake we passed by earlier? A water spirit inches away from drowning a toddler, so it was. These lands are brimming with *mononoke*, with primal hostility, yet he sees none of it. No wonder we Kitsune have transcended, while men remain stuck in the mud."

"But our abilities are much weaker here, so far from our native lands," she replied. "I'm sure you've felt it. This time, there'll be no turning to powerful illusions or strong magic to conjure your way out of trouble."

"No matter. I may be weaker here, but I'm just as clever."

Irony is every spectator's best friend, until it turns suddenly to make a spectacle out of you. While my self-proclaimed "clever" yet hung in the air, a handful of grass sprites halted their squabbling. As a flurry of emerald arrows, they lunged their blade-thin bodies straight for the base of one of the tall oaks lining the road.

The motor screeched to a halt just as the tree crashed across the lane. "These old deathtraps," the driver opined. "Never know when the roots'll give out. Ought to have 'em all torn down and new ones planted."

He wound around the obstruction. The grass sprites stood atop the vanquished trunk, shaking their little fists at us as we passed.

"Could it be that they sense what we truly are?"

Niko asked.

The beast inside of me was throbbing to bare my claws and have at them. But I had a part to play. "Impossible," I said to Niko in frightened accents as I smothered myself upon Edward's chest. "We took great care to disguise our spiritual forms. More likely it's Edward they hate." That most likely hated man patted my head and hushed me with whispers that it was nothing but ill luck, and we were almost there.

"Something's not right, Kyoko," Niko said. "We should leave immediately!"

"Out of the question. I haven't come this far to run home with my tails between my legs." But behind my bravado, uncertainty lurked. Were we upsetting a balance in some way? Bringing our earthly forms to a place where our spiritual forms had no right to be? Or more worrisome: had someone warned them we were coming?

At long last, the motor chugged onto the sprawling grounds of the estate. They stretched as far as the eye could see, manicured lawns and lush flower beds tended by an army of gardeners, a placid river winding into the distance. It was pretty, but far too tame for my more savage tastes, and I was on the verge of disappointment when the spires of Claybury Castle loomed into breathtaking view.

"There you are, darling," Edward cried. "The first glimpse of your new home. What do you think?"

For a moment, I had no words, not even insipid ones. Neither the pictures I'd seen nor the descriptions I'd heard gave justice to the gargantuan scope of the building Edward had the audacity to label with a quaintly "home".

"So big," I whispered, a flushing heat springing to my face. "All mine?"

"Every last inch of it."

I'd never been more aroused. Rectangular in shape and three stories high—though its two dozen or so towers reached yet higher—Claybury Castle eclipsed even the largest castles of Japan. The mansion grew no less impressive as we neared. Hundreds of windows winked from the stonework walls, adorned with scrolls and curls and other carved details.

The motor rounded about a monolithic fountain which stood at the center of the circular drive, spouting elegant arcs of water from the roaring mouths of stone lions, then stopped near the front steps. A tuxedoed man, who I later learned possessed the ridiculously-titled job of "footman", offered his hand to help me out of the motor at the same moment a blur of blonde hair and pale rose muslin careened down the marble front steps, and swallowed Edward in a voluble hug.

"Oh, Edward, Edward, *Edward*! Dearest Edward, you're finally here!"

Lady Arabella was Edward's younger sister and only living relation. He quickly introduced us, and I was peremptorily engulfed in my own crushing hug and outpouring of words.

"Oh Kyoko, Kyoko, *Kyoko*! You must know that you're now as much my sister as Edward my brother, for any woman who can earn the esteem of that wonderful man can only be the truest, most faithful creature to ever be born upon this . . ." Her deluge continued for several tedious minutes, and I wondered briefly if she had somehow transcended the need for breath before she paused, reached into her purse, and produced a small, velveteen box. "I've got them, Edward, just as you asked!"

"Excellent!" he replied. "I knew I could count on you, Bella." He took up the box and and presented it to me. "A welcome home gift."

"For me?" I clapped my hands like a school girl. "What is it, what is it?"

With an impish smile very unlike him, he opened the box to reveal a glinting, ruby bracelet. "This is only part of a

set—" he started before Lady Arabella verbally pushed him aside.

"Yes indeed, for Edward—the dearest soul in the world, but of course I need not tell *you* that—Edward wanted you to wear all of the Caravelle rubies on your first night here, but his steward, stupid man that he is, didn't think it was wise to bring out the whole caboodle just for a dinner at home, so I only fetched the one bracelet out of the safe, and even though it's very fine and practically priceless and will look smashing on you, I do wish you could have worn them all, except for the earrings of course, because you haven't got pierced ears—have you?—and yet I do so hope you will consent to having them pierced, because it's such a sisterly activity and I'm yearning for a bit of companionship after so long alone, and what do you think of it, Kyoko?"

What did I think of it? Edward slipped the bracelet on my arm, where the fat gems shone red as demon's eyes, and I thought that whatever aspersions Niko might have cast about my motives, I was falling more in love with the fool every second it twinkled on my wrist.

"So pretty!" I squealed. "You have more?"

"Oh, yes," she said, "our collection is enormous, one of the largest in the world, and if you ask anyone they'll tell you that we're very distinguished for our immense and diverse collection of gems, and in fact we own certain special, special, *special* pieces that are so old and valuable they haven't seen the light of day in decades and are rumored to no longer exist." She paused to suck in a tremendous breath. "The Eye of Andromeda!" she whispered. "A yellow diamond, over a thousand carats, and set into a necklace worth as much as this house, I tell you! No one's worn it for ages, for we've got it locked, locked, *locked* away in our family safe, where it never leaves, and no one will ever get it, but Edward!—"

Arabella turned ferociously to her brother, eyes wide with abject shock. "Why Edward, it's simply abominable how you've kept your bride idling out here on the drive in this horrid weather, and after such a long, long, *long* journey, when you ought to have led her inside directly and get settled into her room!"

* * *

My "room" as Arabella called it, was more akin to a small palace. Colossal in size, it was a symphony of polished hardwoods and draping silks, haunted here and there by those hints of lace no doubt installed by the ghosts of tight-lipped, crinolined matriarchs.

My trunks were unpacked, the housemaids duly dismissed. A few flicks of the wrist, and my *obi* came untied, my *kimono* a pool of red and gold at my feet.

"At last, I can undress," I said. With my courtly

trappings fallen away, it was time to shed my human ones as well. "This form has been highly uncomfortable, much more than usual."

"It's your own fault," Niko clipped. "If you didn't insist on constructing such intricate disguises, you wouldn't tire yourself so. I could wear this form for ages without undressing."

"In every sense of the word, I imagine." Niko lived in a class of spinsterhood all her own, and I doubt had ever induced a man to anything more amorous than a vague comparison to his mother. But who was I to judge? Ten men, ten colors, as they say, and her insistence on repelling every man who crossed her path only threw me into more desirable relief.

I bent over and arched my back until a thin, pink seam split along the skin of my spine. The fabric of my humanity peeled away as fur the color of maple leaves burst forth, robust and bristling after its long hibernation. Long, black hair retracted into my skull and shaped itself into two triangular ears, while my nose elongated to a black-tipped point. Wiry whiskers sprouted, arms and legs shortened, fingers and toes melded into fuzzy, padded paws until I stood resplendent on all fours.

I hopped lithely onto the vanity, turning this way and that as I inspected myself in the ornate mirror. "As sleek and silken as I remember, and my tails have never looked bushier." For like a flourish on a signature, two gorgeous tails had unfurled, glossy as pearls as I whipped them from side to side.

"Don't get too comfortable," Niko said, picking up the discarded clothes and folding them into neat stacks. "You'll have to transform back soon enough.

Although I suppose now would be a good time to unpack my . . . delicate cargo." She opened my traveling case and carefully lifted out a bowl of rice.

"Niko!" I growled. "Don't tell me you brought—"

"O Divine Inari Okami, your servants summon you, come forth!"

The offering bowl quivered, shook, hummed with a violent, high-pitched note, and finally exploded in a spray of porcelain and noxious declarations:

"My darling Kyoko! Why is that you love nothing more than throwing me into the deepest chasms of despair?"

One would hope that Inari Okami, the immortal rice goddess, would have the decency to shape herself into something presentable. But when the godly attributes were divided amongst the pantheon, Inari Okami was given the barest crumbs of subtlety, and the amorphous, congealed—and suspiciously green-hued—blob hugged the ceiling in a sorrowful pall that rained, quite literally, down over me.

"Must you drip so?" I frowned at the wet splotches spreading along my paws. "I've just given my fur a tongue bath."

She dripped heedlessly on. "Don't speak to me of fur, you heartless child! Why, it was barely a few millennia ago that I raised you up from a mindless vixen wandering the wilds of a newly dawned world. And now here you are, grown up in a wink into a beautiful, young—" She paused, no doubt searching for a word that meant *woman* without quite meaning *woman*. A word that approximated *evil fox demon* without the negative connotations of *evil*, *fox*, or *demon*.

She settled on, "Bride," pronouncing the word as one would *corpse*. "And what must you do, but abandon our native lands and drag me clean across the ocean to this awful, so-called 'England'!"

I lolled my head to the side, the fox equivalent of a shrug. "No one forced you to come here. In fact, I wanted to leave you at home."

"And let you sail away without me to protect you?" she said aghast. "What I don't understand is why you insisted on traveling all the way here. What is it you think you'll find? What is it you seek?"

"Tone down the melodramatics, if you please." I pointed my nose towards the window, where under a swath of moonlight an *amefuri kozou*, garbed in the image of a willowy, skipping boy, had begun molding thunder clouds as a child does a pat of clay. He was soon joined by a dozen or so of his brothers, a herd of ethereal young boys wailing down great sheets of rain. "Your histrionics have summoned our rain bringers all the way from Japan!"

"Not to mention these English spirits don't seem to like us very much," Niko added. "They've already attacked us once. You must be careful, O Starchy One, not to attract any more of our kind from Japan, lest they incite some kind of celestial turf war."

"Too late," I said, for the *amefuri kozou* were approached by a fearsome group of winged, weeping women, English rain nymphs so I surmised, who summarily tackled the *amefuri kozou*, and the two empyreal mobs began wrestling in great peals of thunder and lightning.

"As if those western gods would ever stand a chance against the likes of me!" Inari Okami snorted. Without another word, her blob zipped out the window.

Niko hung her head. "What have we done?"

"There's no use dwelling on what can't be helped. The old girl will tire herself out eventually."

"'Old girl'? You shouldn't speak about her so disrespectfully—"

"Yes, Inari Okami is known for being imminently concerned with respect and decorum," I said, as that deity took aim and flung what was the equivalent of a divine spitball. "Now, do you hear the dinner gong? Difficult to discern over all that tiresome thunder, I know, but it's my cue to change." I flicked my tails side to side. "Chop, chop!"

My fur fractured into countless splinters as Niko disappeared into the large wardrobe. She wrangled me into a corset, then a suffocating gown of pure black which set off my new ruby bracelet like a single star in the night sky.

"All this trickery so you can steal a pretty diamond," she scolded. "If only Inari Okami knew the *real* reason you fled the coop."

"If mischief was a currency, I wouldn't need to steal. Playing tricks and menacing humans doesn't pay the bills, you know."

"You don't have any bills."

"Neither does it put food on the table."

"You don't need to eat!"

"'The weak are meat, and the strong eat' as they say." I fingered the sparkling bracelet on my wrist. Tonight, I would seduce Edward or cajole Arabella into revealing where the family hid their famous jewel. Once an opportunity arose, I'd sniff out the location and have it well in hand. Then Niko and I would sail back home, a thousand times richer and already forgetting these bleak days trapped among English pastures and their spiteful spirits. "Why should the Tengu demons and Ryu dragons be the only ones allowed to gather hoards of pretty trinkets? Our lives are so long, and it'd be dreadfully dull without the distraction of lots of shiny things."

"Do what you will; you always do anyway. But I warn you: make sure you're not the one who gets proverbially eaten."

I patted my coiffure, smoothed down my dress, and with a final glance at the mirror, went to the door. "Don't wait up for me, Niko, and do have fun dining in the servant's hall."

* * *

"Robert," Edward exclaimed, "I'd like you to meet my new wife, Kyoko!"

Robert Callahan, the seventh Viscount of Wyndmouth, bowed. "A pleasure, Lady Ashbourne."

I giggled daintily and proffered him my hand. He took it up in his own, then pressed it against a pair of lips all but suffocating beneath a highly-curled Imperial mustache. Lord Wyndmouth was a boyhood friend of Edward's, so I was told, and his sculpted facial hair and oily manners were a reminder that my endeavor to snag an English lord for a husband could have fared far, far worse.

Although I had assumed dinner on my first night would be an intimate affair, it seemed Edward couldn't resist showing off his little cherry blossom, and his dimples were in full force as he made the rounds, introducing me to half the county, by the looks of it. Though a bevy of unfamiliar faces vied for my attention, it was Lord Wyndmouth's which took center stage. He did everything in his power to commandeer my conversation while we waited to be let in to the dining room, and as a sour plum on top, he was also seated right beside me.

We settled around the long mahogany table. It was clothed in snowy linens, adorned with cut crystal goblets, bone china gilded along the edges in a dense lattice, and an abundance of silver flatware polished so brilliantly it could double as my vanity mirror.

Lord Wyndmouth lifted one of the shining spoons and twirled it through his fingers. "Tell me, Lady Ashbourne, have you been taught the cumbersome rituals of English table etiquette? I find them such a needless amount of ceremony for the simple task of inserting one thing into another." He coughed. "Food into one's mouth, I mean."

'Different body, same mind' as they say. It appeared these English Lords were just as fond of other men's wives as their Japanese counterparts. Never one to let prey out of the trap, no matter how small a catch, I lifted my own spoon in response and touched the smooth, metallic curve to my lips. "You teach me, my Lord?"

"With pleasure. And please, call me Robert."

Empire chandeliers sprinkled an array of shifting light that flirted over the dining guests like desultory butterflies. During our courtship, Edward had boasted of his grand house installed top to bottom with electricity, and the unnatural brightness of this new technology gave one little space to hide. The room was ablaze with blushes, pursed lips, raised eyebrows, and the enthralled gaze of Lord Wyndmouth as the soup was served and he lightly asked:

"How was your passage to England?"

"Long." I held my palms wide apart. "So very long."

"Trapped on a ship for months on end." He took a sip of his dark merlot and licked his lips. "I daresay it must have been a painfully dull affair."

I shook my head with a titter. "Not painful. Don't mind long. Don't mind at all."

"Kept yourself occupied? Yes, I'm sure you and Edward found ways to pass the time." He cleared his throat. "But what an adventure it must have been. Was it your first time riding an ocean liner of that . . . size?"

"First one ever. Never leave home before."

"No, you wouldn't have." He gestured to the floral centerpieces, domes of pink mums and white, hot-house roses. "You were but a bud on the cusp of flowering; now you've arrived, in full and radiant bloom." His nostrils flared and his chest swelled as he inhaled both my physical and metaphorical perfumes. "I can only imagine the courage it took to step aboard that ship. Why, it was only last year that the largest ocean liner ever constructed sank in the Atlantic . . . but perhaps you did not hear of the event?"

The sinking of the unsinkable Titanic was world-wide news that anyone not dwelling in a cave had heard about ten times over. Yet I feigned my usual ignorance: a gracefully-tilted head, lips slightly parted, eyes wide as red-bean pancakes. Only the cleverest of creatures can affect utter idiocy, and my dimwitted mask had been so perfected over the years that at times even I hardly knew where the naive human ended, and the masterminding Kitsune began.

"So sad." I laid a hand over my heart. "My heart break for them."

"As it would to anyone with feeling. For my part, I resolved never again to board an ocean liner, and I hope you won't either. What's the old saying . . . ah, yes: 'an old fox doesn't go twice into the trap'."

"Fox? Trap?" A small tooth of unease gnawed at my interior, but I smothered it with a giggle. "You confuse me, my Lord."

"Now, now. Didn't we agree you'd call me Robert? There's no need to play the innocent with me." He glanced to the head of the table, where Edward sat, red-faced with love and laughter. "'A fox is slyer than ten asses', so they say." Then his eyes flicked down to my wrist, where the rubies likewise glowed, red and bold and pulsing as coals on the fire. "I'm sure you know all about laying traps."

His suggestion upended me. I might have given myself away if Arabella, who sat to his other side, had not then claimed his attention until the final course was consumed, and we ladies repaired to the parlor.

Coffee was served. The ladies unspooled into little coteries of gossip as I ruminated over a cup containing a steaming swirl as black and bitter as my thoughts. Surely all of Lord Wyndmouth's allusions to foxes could not be mere coincidence. Did he know what I was? And if he did, then how?

But these acrid questions, and the acrid beverage, were alike laid aside to seize an opportunity of sidling up to Arabella. No one would approach her for fear of being absorbed in her vortex of words, and she sat apart from us all, in that sort of makeshift isolation one feels when they are alone yet in a room full of people, her eyes staring at nothing, and an unusually cagey look on her face as she aimlessly sipped.

"You tell me about pretty diamond?" I asked her.

She gasped. Porcelain collided with porcelain as she clinked her cup into her saucer. She glanced nervously from side to side and silently mouthed, "The Eye of Andromeda?" The girl would have drawn less attention if she'd stripped down and done the Charleston, and though I wondered how anyone could be this daft by pure accident, I only nodded in reply.

"You show it to me?" I asked.

"Please, my good sister, lower your voice! For you must know that those jewels, and that jewel in particular, have only ever been *rumored* to be in our possession, and if word got out that it is in fact a family heirloom, and kept here at the Castle, there's no telling what kind of thieves and robbers would descend upon these ancestral walls. Besides that, there are strict, strict, *strict* rules concerning its handling, and no one but a direct heir—that means Edward or myself—are even allowed to *touch* the Eye, for my great, great, *great* uncle—who died quite childless—never trusted his nieces and nephews, believing they would snatch it out of his very grave if he went so far as to bury it with him, which indeed he almost did, except that a very adroit salesman talked him instead into purchasing one of his company's safes, and there it has remained to this day."

"Where is safe?"

She pressed a finger into her cheek. "To that, I can't rightly say, and not because I don't know where it is, mind you, but the trouble is describing *where* it is, for all the many twists and turns and secret panels are so, so, *so* difficult to explain, and you must have realized by now that your poor sister has no head at all for words or long explanations, and indeed I do relish the peacefulness that comes from a good, long silence, and so it would be much better if I simply showed you the way myself, but of course that can't happen until this horrid, horrid, *horrid* party leaves, excepting Lord Wyndmouth, of course, who's always been such an upright, honorable sort of man, and I do believe you two were quite engaged with conversation over din—"

She broke off as the gentlemen swarmed in, buzzing with the latent effects of port and cigar smoke.

"A toast!" Edward said, laughing and bidding me to rise. I swanned to his side and he cupped a hand under my chin. "Today, I came home with my bride. And tomorrow," he raised a glass to the crowd, "we hunt!"

The room erupted with a round of *here, here!,* and the distinct rumbles of pleased masculinity into which my surprised soprano could barely make a dent:

"Hunt?"

Edward grinned down at me. "My dear girl, why else have I invited everyone here? Surely I told you all this ages ago. Though I admit the day after our arrival is not the most convenient of times to host a hunt, I never miss opening day—not even for you!" He clapped Lord Wyndmouth on the back. "And neither would Robert! He is our Huntmaster, after all."

"The pursuit," Robert said. "The chase. The hunt. Yes, it is the passion of my life, and always has been."

"What do you hunt?" I asked.

"The only thing worth hunting. That most elusive and cunning of creatures." Robert raised his tumbler and downed the contents in one gulp. "The fox!"

"The only good fox is a dead fox!" Edward chimed in, and at that moment, I felt exactly the same way about husbands. "But darling, what's wrong? You look so pale just now."

"So tired after long journey."

"Of course, of course. What a shocking cad I am, I should never have pushed you on your first night! Why don't you go up to your room and rest?"

I bowed wanly and passed through the room, and as I slipped by Lord Wyndmouth and his prodigious mustache I felt his eyes seared upon me, an old saying bleeding through his toothy grin:

"The brains of a fox," he whispered, "are of little service, when you play with the paw of a lion."

A clack of lightning struck one of the rooftop spires. The electric lights dimmed and flickered as the charge surged through the house, and revelation through my brain, for I finally realized exactly who he was.

Or rather, *what* he was.

"Tanuki!" I hissed under my breath.

* * *

Barbary. Indecency. Savagery.

No, I had not prepared for a fox hunt, and the very idea of it repulsed me from tail to paw. But I said nothing to Niko as I entered my chambers, slipped into bed, and cocooned myself in cashmere blankets and the thorny puzzle of how to piece these unfortunate circumstances into an image of my benefit . . .

"I'm worried about her."

Niko's voice slid surreptitiously into the room's

morning quietude. Dearest Edward must have stayed
up drinking with his hunting friends, for he'd made no
appearance in my bedroom that night, and I shook off
my cogencies, sat up in bed to see her staring somberly
out the window. Rain lathered the panes, and beyond
them Inari Okami and her faithful *mononoke* struggled
against a mounting English army. "She's in trouble,"
Niko said. "She's never left Japan before and has no
idea what these English gods are capable of—neither
do we, for that matter." She strode to the bed. "She's
not at her full strength so far away from home. We
ought to collect her and go home, end this charade
before anyone gets hurt!"

"And we shall, soon. Right after I've got what I came
for. Besides, I'm fairly certain I know who's behind all
our troubles."

"You mean aside from yourself?"

I ignored the barb with a sip. An hour earlier a
breakfast tray had been delivered, loaded with a
steaming teapot filled with what was decidedly not tea.
Oh, it bore a thin verisimilitude, being a brownish
liquid, quite hot, with a handful of tea leaves swimming
at the bottom. But it had been doused with a healthy
measure of milk, then polluted further with two
floating lumps of sugar.

I set down the cup in disgust. "If you must know,
there's a Tanuki afoot. He's disguised, of course, both
his physical and spiritual forms—though he just
couldn't help giving himself away when we met last
night at dinner. He must have come ahead of us, and
set the English spirits against us before we even arrived
in this moldy dishrag of a country."

"Whatever for?"

"Tanuki have always been horrendously jealous of us Kitsune, could never forgive us for being Inari Okami's favorites. That filthy, garbage-picking raccoon probably did it for no other reason than to cause me mischief!"

A knock rattled the door. "Kyoko?" came a familiar, muffled voice. "I'm terribly, terribly, *terribly* sorry to bother you at such an early hour, for you must be monstrously tired after your journey and that utterly taxing dinner, which I must say was rather rude of Edward to schedule on your first night, and . . ."

Niko cracked open the door.

". . . which is why I only buy face creams with mercury, and—oh hello there, Kyoko." Arabella could have been a fish the way she wriggled her way inside and strode briskly to the bed, fumigating the room with prattle as she went. "Anyway, I came to collect the bracelet Edward gave you and take it back to the safe— thought it would be best what with so many, many, *many* people milling around, and Lord Wyndmouth in particular seemed to be around *you* much more than anyone else, which I admit did not surprise me, for I shan't think he'll ever change his ways, just as that old German proverb says, 'the fox changes its fur, but not its habits'."

"Oh?" I regarded her warily, gestured with a languid hand across the room. "Bracelet on vanity."

En route, Arabella paused at the window to gape. "My, but I never did see such weather in all my life, and we had a particularly gruesome, gruesome, *gruesome* storm not three years ago which all but leveled the park, but it was nothing as strange as this!"

Indeed, the scale of the heavenly warfare had

amplified, and now coated the whole landscape with torrential battle. Above, Inari Okami rallied her *amefuri kozou* against the rain nymphs, forming a patchwork of rain and sunshine across the whole sky. Below, a brawl between a *kodama* tree spirit and a nasty-looking dryad shook the woodlands and sent the occasional tree branches plummeting to the ground.

"The whole world looks like it's ending, ending, *ending*! But will they let that cancel the hunt?"

"Hunt?" Niko asked sharply.

"Edward's yearly hunt," Arabella continued, blissfully unaware she'd just lobbed a bomb into the middle of breakfast. "He never misses it, not ever, not even when he's been just married and ought to be catering to his bride's every whim, but that's just like a man, isn't it? To chase, chase, *chase* after the one thing he can't have, when he has something perfectly available right before him, but I've got the bracelet now, dear sister, and so I will leave you to the rest of your morning." She sailed out of the room, bracelet in hand, no regard whatsoever to the gory shrapnel left in her wake.

Niko pounced at once: "You never said anything about a hunt!"

"What with this, that and the whole world ending, ending, *ending,* it must have slipped my mind."

Her eyes narrowed to blades, her words sharp as a scalpel. "What are they hunting?" Leave it to Niko to excise the truth with such merciless precision.

"Foxes."

It was the second explosion of the morning. "And you were just going to stand aside and let it happen?"

"What could I have done?" I argued. "These people

have been hunting foxes for generations; there's no putting an end to it, and these are English foxes, not Japanese."

"As if that should make a difference. Can't you see we must do something about it!"

"But I am doing something. I left my musk on that bracelet, and the scent will lead me straight to the room where they keep the safe. While everyone is occupied with the hunt, I'm going to seize the opportunity and get what I want."

"Even while Inari Okami is out there getting the starch knocked out of her? Even while our very own kind are hunted down like . . . like . . ."

"Like foxes?"

The expression she gave me could shame the makeup off a *geisha*. "How you can lie there in bed making macabre jokes, I'll never know."

I drained my teacup. "'Don't enter the tiger's cage, don't catch the cub'."

"Here's another saying: 'The fox thinks everyone eats poultry like himself'. Well, not everyone does— even other foxes!"

"Calm down, Niko. No need to twist your many tails into a knot." Did I mention she had recently graduated to six tails? Ours, you must understand, is an infernal sort of ranking system, our place in the heavenly hierarchy branded inescapably to our backsides. She was a six-tailed fox, and speeding swiftly towards ascension into a heavenly, golden Kitsune. I was a mere two-tailed, and liable to wallow in my low status till the world crumbled. Our disparity was the eternal rub between us, and the reason I largely scoffed at anything she had to say to me. She always acted so high-handed and superior.

The reason, I believed, our sisterhood would forever be only in name.

"You're one of the oldest Kitsune," she said. "One of the very first Inari Okami ever made. If you'd spent more time helping others, rather than helping yourself to other's possessions, you'd have earned more tails by now!"

"And if you weren't a frightfully self-righteous sycophant, you'd be the one lying in bed while *I* served *you* breakfast."

Niko shrugged into her coat, topped her pinned hair with a straw hat, and strode to the door.

"Do what you like," she said. "I'm going to save them."

"You'll only end up in the hounds' jaws like the rest of them!" I shouted after her.

But she was gone. And I was left alone, save for an empty cup of horrific tea.

* * *

"'Helping others'!" I seethed as I transformed into my fox form. "'Earning more tails'!" Our whole lives, Niko had tried hounding me down a path of her making, then scolded me for not taking it. Couldn't she understand that her desires were not mine? That heavenly ascension was not something I sought?

"I'd rather have one of my tails lopped off than go through the trouble of earning another one!"

I slipped out the door. The halls were deserted. As I suspected, everyone was out attending the hunt. I padded across patterned runners, darted under both new and antique furniture, passed through galleries festooned with more portraits than a museum, all without a soul in sight.

How the world does change! Human senses are so dull. I feel half-blind while parading around as an enfeebled bipedal. But as a fox, another universe gently simmers below human perceptions: midnight sights, distant sounds, the faintest of smells, and the trace scent I'd left on the ruby bracelet emblazoned a pathway as clear as if Bella had painted a line from my bedchamber straight to the safe.

Nose to the floor, the scent led me to a small library in the heart of the west wing, where it dead-ended at a bookcase along the north wall. But here again my supernatural senses aided me, for there was a strong musk emanating from the mantle. Upon investigation, I discovered a pair of levers concealed behind the clock. To pull them, I'd need the use of opposable thumbs. A negligible problem to solve, barring the small detail that I had no clothes on, and thus when I transformed back into Lady Ashbourne, she would be stark naked.

But nothing without risk is worth the doing. With a quick check of the door, Lady Ashbourne burst forth, indulged in a hearty stretch, and then shivered. How humans manage to survive in such thin, frail hides, I'll never comprehend. But primates have their uses, I suppose, for I was able to grasp the levers, and pull.

The bookcase groaned, rumbled, then abruptly parted to reveal a massive safe. This was it. The fruition of everything I'd planned for, schemed for, lied through my teeth for, reveling in every deceitful step along the way, and it was with a thrumming heart and flushed face that I reached for the safe's handle.

"Well, well, well," came a voice from behind. "I think Shakespeare put it best when he said, 'But when the fox hath once got in his nose, he'll soon find means to make the body follow'."

"Lord Wyndmouth." I should have known he'd attempt to thwart the plan. "You've caught me," I said as I slowly turned.

"Or is it the other way around?" His practiced eyes roved up and down my body. "My, but you're not even blushing!"

"Why should I blush?"

"Most ladies in such a compromising position would."

"Except you know for a fact that I'm no lady, don't you?"

"Indeed I do . . ." With that, he loosened his tie, licked his lips, and lunged.

I had no time to transform, to do anything at all but raise my pathetic, clawless arms in defense. But to my surprise, he neither transformed into his raccoon form for an attack, nor used his superior bulk to subdue me. He did nothing at all but lavish me with trails of sloppy kisses and an obscene amount of endearments.

I pushed him off and scrambled backward. "You're no Tanuki!"

He dropped onto his knees, hands clasped before me as a worshiper in earnest prayer. "I confess, I do not know what a Tanuki is, but say the word and I shall endeavor to get it for you!"

No, he was not a Tanuki. The truth of it was much, much worse.

"Dearest Kyoko, end my misery and tell me what

must be done to earn your love!"

I closed my eyes with a sigh. "How did you know I would be here?"

"Edward, of course."

"Edward!"

"Indeed, he told me over billiards late last night that this room was a particular favorite of yours, and that he wouldn't be surprised if you spent all day here while we were out hunting, for you'd no stomach for the sport, especially when foxes were the prey."

"Everyone would be occupied with the hunt, and you decided to seize the opportunity to take what you wanted."

"Exactly so."

"Exactly so . . ." What a perfect fool I'd been. All this time, I'd believed myself the puppet master, the artful hunter. But in truth I was the pawn, caught in a trap of my own making. Outfoxed before setting one foot on this island, while my nemesis stood hidden in plain sight, laughing at me.

Lord Wyndmouth launched himself at me once again, and I pushed him away. "Control yourself, sir! Think of Edward."

This reminder catapulted Lord Wyndmouth into a whirlwind of guilt. "Yes, Edward. The finest friend a man could have. What a cad you must think me, betraying him like this. But I implore you not to count it against me, for the moment I saw you I knew I would do anything to have you."

Outside, another clap of thunder struck.

I smiled. "Anything?"

* * *

Why did you come here?

It was the question posed to me first by Niko, then by Inari Okami. Now, thwarted and humiliated, it was the question I asked of myself.

The question, perhaps, I'd been asking my entire life.

Donned in a black riding habit and skirt, boots that shone as cut obsidian, and a blade-like set to my jaw, I glided outdoors to the stables. I was dressed to kill, but so were they: a score or so of gentlemen milling about in beige breeches and bright scarlet coats, as though they must be clad in the metaphorical pelts of their prey.

"Darling!" Edward boomed as he approached. "We're about to begin the hunt! Surely whatever you need can wait till I return?"

"But I go with you?" I gave a twirl. "Please, I go with you?"

How had I never before noticed his feral grin? "Of course, darling. I shall have the mare saddled at once!"

Footmen burdened with trays wove between the enthusiastic hunters. I plucked a glass of mulled wine and mingled with them as we waited, admiring their horses, praising their attire, puffing them up with the kind of self-deprecating flattery that provokes one into feeling very smart and important, but which over time only serves to transform one into something very stupid and small. The kind of streaming congratulations they'd been showered with all their lives, which was why they never noticed my little hands slipping into their saddlebags.

The chestnut mare was brought out. The steeds

were mounted, the horns blared and the hounds released.

The hunt was on.

We surged down the gravel drive, out of the gates, across the dewy lawns of the park, over the stones of the river bridge to emerge into the wilder pasture lands, where the grass was a thick marble-work of yellows, greens, and browns, and the trees shivered half-naked in the chilled autumn winds. Led by yapping hounds, who in turn were led by the sparks of scents that speckled the chilled English air, the crimson riders spread through the equanimity of the countryside as ripples in a forgotten lake, spilled over the sleeping slopes as though the hills themselves were bleeding.

I rode slowly. Edward was obliged to ride apace with me. In time, we fell behind the others who drove hot on the hounds' heels. The horns became distant echoes, and we were alone: side by side, man and wife, the age-old mortal enemies.

It was time to shed my pretense.

"How long have you hunted foxes?" I asked.

"All my life. It's quite a passion of mine."

"Like Lord Wyndmouth? Is that why you two are such fast friends?"

"Rather not! We're quite different, he and I, for foxes, you understand, are beasts of the chase. There are only two types of men who chase them: those out of love, and those out of hate."

"And which one are you?"

"'The fox's death is the hen's life', as they say. I detest the beasts, and all their ways!"

"What ways are those?"

"Vile, selfish, wicked." He laughed. "But aren't you just full of questions today!"

"More than you know. But I do have one more." I galloped ahead, steered my mare in front of him and then reigned her to a stop, forcing him to halt as well. "Where's the real Edward?" I asked as steel striking flint.

The silly smile that had been his fixture instantly vanished. "Whatever do you mean, *darling*?"

"The man I first met in Japan was indeed Edward Caravelle: young, daft, and charming. You, on the other hand, are nothing short of a fraud, and I want to know what you did with him. Imprison him? Kill him? Eat him?"

"You mean everything *you* would have done to him?"

I bowed. "I see my reputation precedes me."

"Well, well, well." He dismounted, moved to my side with slow, purposeful steps. "If the vixen will finally bare her fangs, I suppose I should, too." His visage flickered. For a brief moment, sharp canines and the smoky shadows of a raccoon mask blurred with his human features. "Don't worry about Edward. I did nothing worse than leave the dolt in Japan under the comfortable hallucination that he's married to a vapid Japanese woman. Not a bad fate, considering the alternative, and I can only wish that I had been half as merciful to myself. But my whole plan hinged on tricking you into marrying me, while making you think it was the other way around."

"Was it?" I said with a yawn, eyes half-lidded. "Or was I tricking you, into thinking that you were tricking me, into thinking that I was tricking you into marrying me?" I looked down my nose on him as I said, "Either way, I'll get what I came for."

"You mean the legendary Eye of Andromeda?" Without warning, he grabbed my hand, pulled me out of the saddle, and kissed me with more heat than he ever had as my husband. "By all means, take it!"

I was more shocked by his invitation than his ardor. "Take it?"

"I couldn't give half a yen for that diamond! This may shock you to hear, but none of this was ever about you or our petty feud. No, this about revenge—not on Kitsune, but on *her*!"

He gestured skyward, where the gods yet battled in sheets of rain and cackles of thunder—and Inari Okami was losing, overwhelmed by their superior numbers, and weakened by the vast distance from the ancient lands whence she drew her power.

"She always favored you," Edward went on. "Always considered Kitsune her prized children, the most clever and the most loyal, while we Tanuki were relegated to the bottom of the pack." He threw back his head and laughed. "Well, she's no longer a big fish in a small pond, is she? I told those English gods and spirits that a foreigner was on her way to stir up trouble, and the old girl played beautifully into my plan. Now Inari Okami will learn what a mistake it is to ignore us. And you . . ." His eyes, once light as air, were dark as moonless waters. "You'll live the rest of your long, pathetic life humbled by the fact that a Tanuki has outfoxed you. That I've outfoxed the fox!"

Why did you come here?

In that moment, I had no answers, save for one:

"One thing you've got wrong: I didn't come here for

the jewels. It's not the diamond I truly seek."

"And what is?" he sneered. "Compassion for man? Honor amongst your kind? Ascension to the heavens, where you can snivel before Inari Okami for eternity?"

"Nothing so noble, I'm afraid. We're far too alike for that. You see, I've already taken the diamond, and all the other jewels stashed in the safe. I slipped them into your friends' saddlebags, then slipped a word into an *amerfuri kozou's* ear—you know what gossips they are —that the greatest hoard to be had on this earth was right here in a little place called Leicester, England— and now look *there!*"

I pointed eastward. It was only a dimple at first, a small, black smudge along the horizon. An angry mass drawing closer, close enough to discern the swirls and writhing shapes, the army of foreboding creatures wading through the sky.

"The Ryu and the Tengu," he whispered, eyes wide and face white.

"Yes," I said. "The dragons and the demons. The great *mononoke* who love wealth even more than a Kitsune, and by the gods, they've come to claim it!"

The Ryu dragons bore down first, their serpentine bodies twisting and undulating, encouraging great gales to whip through the air and shatter across the grasslands. The Tengu followed suit, flapping giant feathered wings that blocked out the sun, and throwing slicing winds headlong upon the earth. Limbs were shorn from trees and the ground vibrated as those almighty spirits chased after the jewel-laden saddlebags. With Ryu claws and Tengu beaks snapping at their backs, the hounds and riders retreated back to the manor, the hunters now turned prey. Inari Okami's army had doubled in size and strength, and she led a renewed assault that agitated the weather from a mild temper tantrum, into a paroxysm of fury.

A bloom of funnel clouds touched down, flinging leaves, sticks, the occasional sheep, and anything else in their path.

"Time to leave, I think." I transformed into my fox form, scurried off, and dove into the safety of a nearby burrow, leaving Edward to gape at his carefully-laid plans evaporating like morning dew.

Eventually, the howling winds died, and I poked my nose out of the burrow mouth. Sunlight shone over the murdered landscape. The roaring clouds dissipated, and Inari Okami wafted gently to the ground, arm linked with some kind of English spirit.

The war, it seemed, was over.

A skulk of foxes emerged from the brush, one of them looking slightly more sanctimonious than the others.

"Niko!" I ran up and licked her face. "How is it you tell me to take care that I'm not the one to get eaten, then go throwing yourself straight into the maws of the hounds?"

"I did only what needed to be done. But that was a rather tidy trick you pulled, bringing over our heavy hitters to save Inari Okami, and chase all these nasty hunters away."

"Not all of them!"

Niko didn't see the pounce coming, but I did. Edward, now garbed in his proper Tanuki form, lunged with razored jaw straight for my sister's throat.

"Niko!" I leapt between them, and his teeth plunged into my shoulder. Red blood blended into my fur as he shook me in his jaws, then released me with a jerk of his head. I flew out of his mouth and skidded across the ground, limp, bloodied, bruised—but still with a careless chuckle on my lips.

"What are you laughing at?" Edward growled.

"You. Us. How deep down, we're exactly the same."

"I'm nothing like you!"

"Of course you are. Petty, vain, and out for revenge!"

I sprung into the air with bared teeth and tackled him to the ground, and together we tumbled in a throbbing ball of fur and tooth and claw. But Tanuki, in terms of brute strength, outclass us Kitsune, and he soon had me pinned beneath him with all fours.

Blood dripped from his canines and splashed onto the white fur of my face. "You could never go toe-to-toe against me!"

"You're right, which is why I've brought backup."

"TANUKI!"

The single word ripped though the brush, quickly followed by a bedraggled, mustached Lord Wyndmouth. He bore a wild tang in his eyes and a ferocious shotgun in his arms—which he aimed directly at Edward.

"You're the creature which Lady Ashbourne requires to return my love!" he cried.

Edward scrambled away from Lord Wyndmouth's bead. "What's that fool doing here?"

I rolled back to my feet and bounded away. "I may have confessed to him that all I wanted in the whole world was a Tanuki pelt," I said, "and that I had seen one roaming about the wood not last evening."

"I'll rip him to shreds!"

"No doubt." The crack of a shotgun blast rang out. "But you'll have to dodge his bullets first!"

As Lord Wyndmouth chased my yelping dog of a husband through the bracken, Niko loped up to me, nudged me gently with her nose. "You're hurt!"

"A few scratches, perhaps. Nothing Inari Okami can't deal with in a snap. Now where did she fly off to?"

We trotted over to where I'd seen Inari Okami land and lo, there she sat, chatting with an English goddess like they'd been friends all their lives.

"So good of you to call for that truce," Inari Okami said to her. "Not right for us to fight so, when really it's those humans who cause us the most trouble—oh, but here come my daughters!" She flinched at my bloodied face and shoulder. "Dearest Kyoko, have you been fighting again?" She showered me in a golden, healing rain. "I tell her over and over to leave the poor Tanuki alone, but does she listen?"

"Oh, they never listen!" The other goddess tossed back her hair of golden wheat. "Why, my favorite daughter once ran off to the underworld with a simply dreadful man, a wretch of a devil who reeked of brimstone, all so she could get a few seeds of a pomegranate. As if we didn't have pomegranates right at home! To say nothing of all my children who've up and run off to that godforsaken America."

"America?" Inari Okami gasped in horror. "I'd never forgive it!"

The pair continued their discourse with hushed tones and bent heads, talking about us as though we weren't even there.

"I know I shouldn't say it," Niko whispered to me, "but grain goddesses are a bit glutinous, aren't they?

Never happier than when they're stuck together, gossiping."

I'd never been prouder of her in my life, nor felt more like her sister. "Now who's the disrespectful one?"

* * *

I placed the jewel case into Arabella's arms. "I thought it would be safer with you than back in the safe."

"Yes, now that everyone knows our family possesses the Eye of Andromeda, I imagine we shall be beset by all kinds of thieves and swindlers and charlatans, and I'm not sure what I would have done if you had not been there to safeguard it during that ghastly storm, for it was nothing but chaos in the house, and I don't think I've ever met anyone as honest and true as you, dear Kyoko!"

I cleared my throat. "I do what I can."

"You do more than that." She grasped my hands. "Indeed, it's unaccountable why Edward has run off like this, and though I know his abandonment is far too cruel for you to forgive, blood is thicker than water, as they say, and I'm, determined, determined, *determined* to find him and bring him back home!" She sighed. "Though I do wish I could say the same for Lord Wyndmouth."

"Let Lord Wyndmouth go, Arabella. I know his kind and he's not worth the trouble. Forget about him."

"I wish I could. I've tried ever so hard, but he's been firmly lodged in my heart ever since we were children, and no matter how much of cad he is, I can't seem to rid myself of him."

"Perhaps not. But you've got youth and a priceless diamond on your side." I nudged her onto the gangplank. "Who knows what might happen on a long sea voyage?"

She vanished into the belly of the ship just as another passenger came to stand beside me.

"I'm astonished you gave her the diamond back," Niko said. "And proud," she added at my frown.

"There's plenty more trinkets out there, and I think she needs it more than I do." We stood side by side on the faded, warped dock, our faces to the sea. "So you really won't go with me?" I asked.

She patted her traveling case. "I must take Inari Okami back to Japan. Not to mention the small matter of freeing a certain English lord from a certain hallucination."

"So you'll make sure Arabella finds the real Edward?"

"Of course."

"Though I wonder whether you should bother. Sounds like he's living out his wildest dream."

"And are you living yours?" Her hard features softened minutely, and gave the faint impression that there was a heart pulsing somewhere beneath that immutable, glass-like exterior. "You were right in saying that you and the Tanuki were alike."

"Bite your tongue, or I'll bite it for you."

"But it's true. Flip sides of the same coin, isn't that what they say? A *mononoke's* life is long. Whether Tanuki or Kitsune, some of us aren't content to go about doing good deeds for eternity. No, some of us need adventure, a chase, always something new to seek after."

"Perhaps you're right."

The waters turned, the currents raged. The drops of water that fall from the sky never live in the same place twice. They swim through seas and fly through clouds, travel the world a hundred times over, yet are never content to settle down, and as Niko boarded a boat bound for Japan, I was left on shore, alone once more with The Question:

Why did I come here?

With the ocean a red carpet, the whole world my oyster, and a rumor swirling that there were some fantastically rich men aboard another ocean liner, I stepped up to the ticket counter with a smile, for I finally had my answer:

For the hunt!

"One first class ticket to New York City!"

––––––––––

Long ago Mei Davis left the technical world to become a full-time mom and sometimes-writer. She lives in Detroit, Michigan with her husband, children, and a large, cannibalistic goldfish.

FIN